friends, cooking, eating, talking, life.

Grosset

For Jamie Muldrow—D.M.

Special thanks to Kari Muldrow, Jim Muldrow,
Song Gu Muldrow,
and the real Peichi—Peichi Tung

dish #3

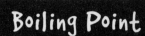

Boiling Point

friends, cooking, eating, talking, life.

By Diane Muldrow

Illustrated by Barbara Pollak

Grosset & Dunlap
New York

GROSSET & DUNLAP
Published by the Penguin Group
Penguin Group (USA) Inc., 375 Hudson Street, New York, New York 10014, U.S.A.
Penguin Group (Canada), 90 Eglinton Avenue East, Suite 700, Toronto, Ontario,
Canada M4P 2Y3 (a division of Pearson Penguin Canada Inc.)
Penguin Books Ltd, 80 Strand, London WC2R ORL, England
Penguin Ireland, 25 St Stephen's Green, Dublin 2, Ireland
(a division of Penguin Books Ltd)
Penguin Group (Australia), 250 Camberwell Road, Camberwell, Victoria 3124,
Australia (a division of Pearson Australia Group Pty Ltd)
Penguin Books India Pvt Ltd, 11 Community Centre, Panchsheel Park,
New Delhi - 110 017, India
Penguin Group (NZ), Cnr Airborne and Rosedale Roads, Albany, Auckland 1310,
New Zealand (a division of Pearson New Zealand Ltd)
Penguin Books (South Africa) (Pty) Ltd, 24 Sturdee Avenue, Rosebank,
Johannesburg 2196, South Africa

Penguin Books Ltd, Registered Offices:
80 Strand, London WC2R ORL, England

2007 Edition
Cover photos © Blend Images, LLC

Text copyright © 2002 by Diane Muldrow. Interior illustrations copyright ©
2002 by Barbara Pollak. All rights reserved. Published by Grosset & Dunlap, a
division of Penguin Young Readers Group, 345 Hudson Street, New York, New York
10014. GROSSET & DUNLAP is a trademark of Penguin Group (USA) Inc. Printed in
the U.S.A.

The Library of Congress has cataloged the original edition
[ISBN 0-448-42828-8] as follows:
Library of Congress Control Number: 2002102955

ISBN 978-0-448-44528-1   10 9 8 7 6 5 4 3 2 1

BRRRIIING!

"Phone!" called Molly Moore, who was sliding a cookie sheet out of the oven. "Can somebody get it? I have to get these cookies out of the oven before they're totally ruined!"

BRRRIIING!

"*Gross!* This package of chicken is dripping!" cried Peichi Cheng. "Yuck! It's leaking all over the place."

BRRRIIING!!

 "*Aaah!* I dropped another egg on the floor!" groaned Shawn Jordan.

BRRRIIING!!

"Oh, *I'll* get the phone!" shouted Molly. She dropped the cookie sheet down on the counter and raced toward the phone.

"Got it!" called out Molly's twin, Amanda. She skidded down the hall into the Moores' kitchen and grabbed the receiver. Amanda had a weird talent of *always* getting the phone before Molly did.

"Hello?" said Amanda, out of breath. "This is Amanda Moore...Right. Yes, we've cooked for a few people. We

have a new business called Dish. We cook five nights'
worth of dinners and deliver them—"

Molly, Shawn, and Peichi gasped. Amanda looked over
at her sister and friends with her eyes wide, her head
nodding, as if to say *Can you believe this?*

Just then, a large metal spoon slipped off a counter
and fell to the floor with a loud *clang*.

"—Um, we deliver the food to you," continued
Amanda, distracted. "Oh, you only need it for three
nights? Well, we could do that, too. That'll cost less, of
course...okay...what would we make? Well, we make
basic stuff, like, we could roast a chicken for you, make
some homemade macaroni and cheese, some pesto sauce
for pasta, stuff like that...for Thursday? I just need your
name, address, and phone number. Okay. Thank you. We'll
see you then. Bye."

She hung up. "Guess what, Chef Girls? We have
another cooking job!"

"*Yesss!*" cried the girls.

"Dish *rocks!*" said Molly, as she gave
her sister a high-five. "Who was that? And
how did they hear about Dish? Here, help
me take these cookies off the cookie
sheet or they'll keep baking."

"*Mmmm,* chocolate chip," said Amanda as she
reached for a spatula. "I wish these were for us."

"We can keep a few aside," said Molly with a sly

smile. "We didn't promise our customers an entire batch! We just said we'd include 'some cookies.'"

The twins heard the front door open.

"Cookies!" shouted their seven-year-old brother, Matthew. He came running down the hall and into the kitchen. "I could smell 'em outside!"

"Don't slide in the chicken mess!" cried Peichi. She held her arms out wide like a traffic cop.

"Watch the egg!" said Shawn, who was wiping off the floor. "And don't step on my hand, Matthew."

"Wow, you guys are making a mess. Mom's gonna be mad!" said Matthew. He stood as close as he could to the counter without stepping into the goo on the floor, and reached for a cookie.

"*Gross!* Your hands are *filthy*," cried Molly. "Wash them. *With soap.*"

Matthew hated to be told what to do by his big sisters, but this time the payoff was too good. So he crossed the Moores' big kitchen to the sink and washed off the crusty dirt.

"How'd your hands get so dirty, anyway?" asked Molly, wrinkling her freckled nose. "Get the paper towels for Peichi while you're over there."

"I don't know," said Matthew with a shrug. "Say 'please.'"

"*Please* bring the paper towels for Peichi," said Molly with a sigh.

"Dirt just finds him, no matter what he's doing," joked Amanda.

"He gets dirty just sitting in church," added Molly.

"Ha, ha, you're so funny," said Matthew. "Go long, Peichi!" He tossed the fat paper towel roll like a football to Peichi. It headed way too close to a ceramic cookie jar. Luckily, Peichi caught it.

"*Oof!*" cried Peichi. "Gee, *thanks*, Matthew," she said, rolling her eyes. Matthew held up his arms in victory and made sounds like a screaming crowd of sports fans.

Both Molly and Amanda closed their eyes and let out sighs of relief. They opened their eyes to see Matthew grabbing as many cookies as his small hands could hold.

"Hey, slow down!" cried Molly.

"These are for Ben, too," Matthew explained, balancing eight warm, gooey cookies in his hands. Ben was Matthew's best friend. He lived across the street. The two had been inseparable since the boys were babies. And Ben's mom, Mrs. Bader, was Matthew's official baby-sitter.

"Well, so much for a few cookies for *us*," said Amanda, as Matthew slammed the front door shut.

"Who was on the phone, anyway?" asked Shawn.

"Someone named Mrs. Jamison. She lives on Fifth Street. She heard about our cooking from Mrs. Lawlor. I guess Mrs. Lawlor really liked the food we cooked for her after she got out of the hospital. Mrs. Jamison is having some sort of women's group over, and she wants some fun snacks. The next day, she's going on a business trip. Her husband can't cook at all, and she has two little kids."

"I can't believe we got another call," said Shawn, shaking her head. "Here we are, doing a cooking job *today* for the Falvos—"

"I know!" cried Peichi. "I mean, we just decided to try to turn our cooking club into a little business, and our parents *finally* allowed us to do it, and Dish is taking off by itself. We haven't even made flyers yet, or put an ad in the paper!"

"Right," said Molly. "It's almost happening without us. We really don't have Dish together yet. We're not— we're not—"

"Organized," said Amanda. "Well, guys, that's what we have to work on. As soon as we can! In between cooking jobs."

BZZZ!

"Phone!" shouted Peichi.

"That's not the phone," Molly said with a laugh. "It's the kitchen timer. The chicken's done."

"Can I just say how awesome we are for cooking something this good?" said Shawn, as she carefully took the chicken out of the oven.

"*Mmmmm*," sighed the girls all at once.

The girls had bought three pounds of chicken tenders, which they'd seasoned with teriyaki sauce, balsamic vinegar, fresh basil, and tarragon, the way Mrs. Moore had taught them. And it smelled unbelievable!

"Wow!" cried Peichi. "*This* is what I want for dinner tonight. It smells so good!"

"That's from the herbs we put on it," said Shawn. "But how do I know if it's done?"

"It *looks* done," said Peichi. "It's nice and brown, anyway."

"Just cut open a piece," said Molly, reaching for a knife.

"No! Don't do that!" cried Shawn. "It won't look pretty."

"No big," said Molly.

"I can't look!" cried Shawn, hiding her eyes. "She's ruining my chicken!"

Molly carefully sliced through part of a plump piece of chicken and prodded open the meat. "It's still too pink," she said. "Right, guys?"

The girls leaned over and peered at the chicken. "The recipe says it's done when the juices run clear," said Amanda, who'd quickly scanned a page in Mom's favorite cookbook. "This needs to go back in."

Shawn put her oven mitts back on and opened the

oven door. She slid the glass pan full of chicken back in the oven and closed the door. "I hope I don't end up burning it," she said. "What if it gets too tough?"

"Don't worry," said Amanda. "We can just stick the meat thermometer in a piece of chicken. When it reads one hundred eighty degrees, the chicken will be done."

"We should have thought of using it earlier—before we mangled this poor bird!" Shawn said.

Amanda shrugged. "Well, we can't think of *every-thing*. The chicken will look and taste just fine!"

Besides the chicken, the girls had also made home-made macaroni and cheese, a tomato sauce for pasta, a pasta salad, a chickpea salad, a cold soup called gazpacho, scalloped potatoes, and the cookies. The woman whom they were cooking for, Mrs. Falvo, had asked for some-thing for breakfast, too, so the girls had made banana bread. Some of the dishes the girls made were from family recipes, and some were from their weekly cooking class that they had been taking together.

"My legs are stiff," groaned Molly. She plopped into a chair at the Moores' kitchen table. "*Aaaahhh.*"

"So are mine," said Shawn, pulling out a chair. Amanda and Peichi did the same.

It felt good to sit down, which none of them had done in hours.

Molly looked around the big kitchen. She and

Amanda spent a lot of time in there—more time than in the room they shared. And lately, Peichi and Shawn had been spending a lot of time there, too. The kitchen was inviting and open, with its high ceilings, pale yellow walls, and deep blue and green tiles that Mom had found in Spain. It was decorated with funky old dishes and bowls, colorful rugs shaped like apples and pears, and gleaming copper pots that hung from the ceiling. It was a place in which to hang out, do homework, and talk to Mom while she cooked. Mom cooked a lot on the weekends. Dad pretended to help, but he really just enjoyed spending time with Mom in the kitchen, too.

"Hey, Molls, do you think we have enough containers?" Amanda asked, looking at all the food.

Molly just continued staring into space.

"Yo, Molly!" Shawn called.

"Molls, this is no time to daydream. We have a ton of work to do," Amanda said.

"Huh?" Molly said, blushing. "I-I heard you."

"Yeah, right," Amanda said.

"Molly, do you think we have enough containers for all this food?" Shawn asked, stepping in between the girls.

Molly stood up. "No problem. We have plenty in here." She opened up a cabinet.

"I can't wait to get paid!" Peichi said as the girls started to pack the food away.

"We're going to be extra-rich this week, because we have to turn around and start cooking for the Jamisons!" Shawn pointed out. "Oops, I forgot—we should finish paying back Grandma Ruthie."

Shawn's grandmother had loaned Dish the money to buy a secondhand fridge that was kept in the Moores' basement. Now the girls could keep the food for their jobs out of Mrs. Moore's way.

"We need to come up with a plan to pay back Grandma Ruthie," Amanda said. "But right now we need to figure out when we should go shopping for the Jamison job. Tomorrow morning? Molly and I have piano lessons tomorrow afternoon."

"Tomorrow morning doesn't work," said Peichi. "I have my flute lesson, and I'm so not ready."

"Well, tomorrow morning's the only time that works for me," Shawn said.

"That's okay," said Peichi. "We don't all have to go every time, do we?"

"I guess not," said Molly.

"Well, let's get going!" said Peichi. "Let's walk this food over to the Falvos'! Then we'll head over to my house and go swimming."

"Uh, Peichi, the chicken's still in the oven," said Shawn.

"Oh, yeah." Peichi blushed as she sat down.

"We really should just go shopping after we drop off this stuff," suggested Amanda.

Everyone groaned.

"I wanna go swimming!"

"Me, too."

"We worked all day! We need a break."

"Guys, it's just food shopping. We can swim afterwards!"

"All right," the girls agreed

To: mooretimes2
From: qtpie490
qtpie490: wuzzup, M & A?
mooretimes2: not much, Shawn, wuzzup with u? We're tired from cooking and shopping and swimming today.
qtpie490: me too! Hey can u meet me 2morrow morning at the park?
mooretimes2: where? The usual place?
qtpie490: yup, Turtle Bench.
mooretimes2: ok, what 4?
qtpie490: I need 2 talk!
mooretimes2: did something bad happen?
qtpie490: not really. Don't worry. GTG! See u at 10. Mwa!
mooretimes2: ok. b-b <3 <3 <3 <3

After Molly and Amanda logged off the computer they went upstairs to their big pale-blue room. It had twin beds, a window seat, and a full-length mirror that Molly teased Amanda for spending too much time in front of. The window seat had a dark blue cushion littered with dozens of stuffed animals. The twins didn't really play with them anymore, but getting rid of them was unthinkable.

Amanda began to brush her hair. Molly sat on the window seat and hugged her old pink elephant. "I wonder what's up with Shawn?" she asked, trying to sound casual.

Amanda shrugged. "I don't know," she said. "The suspense is killing me!"

"Me, too," admitted Molly. She sighed. "I just hope Shawn's okay."

chapter 2

Molly woke up early. Their tall row house was quiet. Taft Street was quiet. But something had woken her up. She turned her head in the direction of a cooing pigeon outside on the windowsill. There was Matthew's fat tiger cat, Kitty. She'd jumped noisily onto the windowsill and was staring intently at the bird.

"Kitty," whispered Molly, "that bird isn't afraid of you."

Kitty turned to look at Molly and jumped right onto her stomach.

"*Oof!*" Molly said, trying not to wake up Amanda, who was sound asleep.

Molly looked at the glowing red numbers on her alarm clock. Six-thirty A.M. It was still hours before she and Amanda were to meet Shawn.

As Molly petted Kitty, she wondered what the deal was with Shawn. Shawn had been Molly's and Amanda's best friend for years, and they'd seen her through a lot. When Shawn's mother died a few years ago, after a long illness, Molly and Amanda were there for her. Having sleepovers. Bringing her along to their grandpa's house on the Jersey Shore. And just hanging out. Shawn was an only child, and Molly and Amanda were like sisters to her.

Oh, I know what this is about, Molly suddenly realized. *I think.*

A few hours later, the twins were waiting for Shawn at Turtle Bench in Prospect Park, watching two swans glide silently through the water.

It had been only recently that the twins' parents and Shawn's dad let them go to the park without them. Prospect Park was huge and thickly wooded, so the girls couldn't just roam anywhere they wanted to. But they *were* allowed to hang out in small sections of the park right near their homes. Now that the girls were eleven, their parents had given them a little more freedom. They could explore the cool toy stores, bookstores, and pizzerias of their neighborhood, Park Terrace, Brooklyn, as long as they were in a group of two or more.

Sometimes the girls visited the seals and other animals at Prospect Park's new zoo. Nearby was a cool old carousel. The big lake had pedal boats, and there were beautiful meadows everywhere for picnics. Free plays, dance performances, and concerts were held at the band shell all summer long. And there was ice-skating at the rink all winter. Near the park stood the huge Brooklyn Public Library, the Brooklyn Museum of Art, and the Brooklyn Botanic Garden. If this wasn't enough, Manhattan was only a quick subway ride away. The girls loved living in New York.

"We always get here before Shawn," Molly told Amanda. "Did you ever notice that?" She pulled her long brown hair into a high ponytail.

"That's 'cause Shawn just lives over there," said Amanda, pointing to a tall apartment building. "So she always leaves at the last minute." Amanda held up her hand and inspected her glittery lavender fingernails. "You should try this color, Molls. Your nails look terrible. Are you biting them again?"

Molly blushed. "I guess I am."

Amanda rolled her eyes. She was the fashion conscious sister. Amanda loved clothes, jewelry, nail polish, lip gloss...it seemed that every week, she was trying a new nail polish color or hairstyle. Molly, on the other hand, loved a comfortable old pair of jeans and boys' canvas sneakers. She spent her allowance on CDs and hardly ever bought anything like lip gloss or hair accessories. "What's the point?" she would tell Amanda, whenever Amanda begged her to buy something girly. "You already have all that stuff. I'm not wasting *my* money."

The twins were different in other ways, too.

Amanda was cautious. Molly loved doing things on the spur of the moment, and always had a big idea she wanted to try out. Cooking had been her idea one boring day earlier in the summer. The twins were tired of all the take-out food their parents had been bringing home lately.

"Let's cook dinner!" Molly had suggested. Despite Amanda's protests, they did, and it tasted great! That led to their summer adventures—taking cooking classes in the neighborhood, getting to know Peichi better, and...starting their own cooking business—Dish! None of that would have happened if Molly hadn't decided to take a risk.

"Here she comes," said Molly, as she watched Shawn walk under some trees that bordered the lake.

Shawn was wearing denim shorts, running shoes, and her new candy-striped peasant top. Her bright green "cat glasses" looked so great against her coffee-colored skin. They were the same color as one of the stripes in her top. Shawn always looked—and acted—and dressed—so cool. Who else could pull off wearing really out-there eyeglasses? Or stay calm in the most bizarre situations?

Only Shawn. Amanda wanted to dress like her, and Molly wanted to act like her. But they never really could. Shawn was one-of-a-kind.

"Hi, Molls," said Shawn. "Hi, Manda."

"Hi," said the twins. "What's up, Shawn?" they both asked at the same time, and then giggled. They did that all the time—"the twin thing"—when they said the same thing at the same time.

"Did you see any turtles yet?" asked Shawn, ignoring the question. She stared at the water. "My dad and I did, yesterday."

"Okay, Shawn, give it up," said Molly. "Tell us what's going on."

Shawn sighed and sat down on the grass in front of the bench so that she could look at the twins.

"Um, okay. Here it is. Remember that long business trip my dad's been talking about? Well, he's going on it after all. He's going to Australia and New Zealand." She looked down at the ground. "Wherever that is!" she said with a little laugh. "No, I know where it is. On the other side of the world!"

"I had a feeling this was happening," said Molly. "How long is he going to be away?"

"A month."

"Whoa!" exclaimed Molly. "That's a long time!"

"I was bummin' when he told me," said Shawn, shaking her head.

"That *is* a bummer," said Amanda. "So, like, what are you going to do?"

"I know!" Molly broke in. "You can live with us! It would be so cool—like a month-long slumber party!"

Shawn smiled a little smile. "Thanks," she said. "But, um—I'm gonna go back down to South Carolina and stay with Grandma Ruthie. For the rest of the summer." She looked at Molly, then her eyes flicked over to Amanda.

"What!" cried the twins.

"But you just got *back* from there," said Molly. "You were there at the beginning of the summer, and it seemed like you were gone forever. You just got home!"

"I've been back for a while," said Shawn softly.

"But Shawn, we're all having such a great time," declared Amanda. "This summer is *awesome*. We're just getting Dish going. And we're writing our cookbook. Why do you want to leave?"

"I don't really *want* to leave," replied Shawn with a shrug. "But what else can I do?"

Molly stared at Shawn. So did Amanda. Then the twins glanced at each other, and realized that they were both wondering the same thing: *Does Shawn even care that she's leaving?*

Molly forced a smile as she turned to Shawn. "Well, why can't Grandma Ruthie come *here*?"

"Grandma Ruthie doesn't want to be up here that long," said Shawn. "I already asked her. And, well, I'm not gonna lie to you guys. I like it down there. I love going to Myrtle Beach with my cousins. I've been having a lot of fun here, too. You know that, right? But..."

A large dark cloud passed over the sun, and the air suddenly felt cold. Molly shivered.

"But it's just better this way," continued Shawn. "Okay? Anyway, I'll be leaving in a few days. It's just for a month, guys."

Neither Molly nor Amanda knew what to say.

Shawn was acting weird. A little *too* cool.

Suddenly it seemed to the twins that Shawn had already checked out. And gone.

chapter 3

That night, when Mrs. Moore came home from work, she found the twins in the garden. "Hi!" she said. She kissed them and asked, "Do you want to eat dinner out here tonight?"

"Okay," replied Molly.

"Sure," Amanda mumbled.

"Something's up with you two," stated Mrs. Moore. "What's going on? You seem so glum."

"What does 'glum' mean?" asked Amanda.

"If it means bummed out, then we're glum all right," said Molly. "We're 'glummed out.'" She snickered at her little joke.

Mom set down her heavy bag. "What's up?" she asked.

The twins told Mom all about their talk with Shawn.

"I see," said Mom. "I'm sorry you're going to be missing Shawn all over again."

"And it doesn't sound as if she'll miss *us*," Molly blurted out.

"Oh, that's not true," Mrs. Moore assured the girls. "But try to remember that other than her dad, Shawn

19

doesn't have any family here in New York. Sometimes it's just good to be with your family. That seems to be what Shawn needs right now. And she likes it down in South Carolina, so it's not sad for her to go there."

Mrs. Moore smiled at her daughters. "That doesn't mean she won't miss you, and all the fun you're having," she went on. "But growing up is about accepting things that you can't change, and making choices that are right for yourself. And Shawn's doing pretty well in that area. Losing her mother has forced her to grow up. Try to see it her way. And try not to make it harder for her, okay?"

The twins didn't say anything for a while. They were thinking about everything Mom had said. It was a lot to take in. But it did seem to make sense.

"Well," said Molly slowly, "I guess I haven't really looked at this the way Shawn would."

"Me, either," said Amanda. She sighed. "Okay, Mom. She's here for a few more days, so Molly and I will—"

"Just act normal and not make her feel guilty!" interrupted Molly.

Mom smiled again. "Shawn's lucky to have you two as her best friends."

"*Cha-ching! Cha-ching!*" cried Molly, the next afternoon. The friends had just dropped off their latest cooking job at Mrs. Jamison's house.

"Peichi, we'll divide the money at your house," Amanda said, pocketing the wad of bills Mrs. Jamison had just given them.

"You know what's really fun?" asked Peichi. "When we open up the boxes and show the customer what we made for them—"

"And their eyes bug out and they say how good it all looks!" interrupted Amanda.

"Mrs. Jamison looked so surprised when she saw how young we are," commented Shawn. "Everybody's like that at first. And then they see what we did, and they're so impressed. That's, like, just as good as getting paid."

"Mrs. Jamison wouldn't have been so impressed if she'd seen us outside her door, right after we rang the bell," said Molly. "I'm still shaking!"

"I still can't believe you and Peichi almost spilled that whole platter of mini-pizzas," Amanda reminded them. "What a mess that would've been!"

"You're telling me!" Peichi said with a giggle. "Come on, let's walk faster! I can't wait to show you my new room!"

"You've been saying that all day," Molly teased her.

Amanda stopped to fix the strap of her sandal that had slipped down. "I have to get another hole in this strap. It's too loose," she said.

"Come on! Come *on*!" Peichi said impatiently. "You can fix your shoe at my house."

The girls knew Peichi was excited, so they hurried the rest of the way to her house.

"Everybody close your eyes!" said Peichi as she led the friends upstairs to her room. "I mean, after you get upstairs."

She opened her door. "*Ta-da!*" she cried.

"*Oooh!*" squealed the girls.

Mrs. Cheng had painted the room ivory. A large cotton chenille rug, also in ivory, made the room look cozy. Sheer ivory drapes hung from the tall windows. In one corner was a new white wooden desk, with cute little cubbies and drawers, and a matching white chair with an aqua velvet cushion. In another corner was an overstuffed armchair, upholstered in aqua velvet. A dresser matched the desk. On the floor were four gigantic velvet pillows for sitting on—in aqua leopard print!

But the best thing was Peichi's queen-sized wooden sleigh bed.

"It's my parents' old bed," explained Peichi. "They got a new bed. This is so huge, I feel like I'm in a boat!"

"We could all have a sleepover right *here!*" Molly joked, plopping on the bed.

Peichi had picked out the bedding herself. Her friends loved the aqua puffy quilt. It was bordered in velvet, in a very pale aqua. Two matching pillow shams completed the look.

There were fun touches, too—a groovy pink Lava Lamp. Transparent yellow plastic towers for CDs. Even a string of white lights with pink plastic flower-shaped covers.

There was also a traditional touch. Under glass, hanging on a wall, was a woman's black Chinese silk jacket with colorful embroidery. It had belonged to Peichi's grandmother, Ah-mah.

"Wow! Your parents went *all out!*"

"I love your bed!"

"I love how bright everything is. Can I move in?"

Shawn ran her hand over the quilt's silky fabric as she gazed around the room. "I love it, Peichi," she said. "Now I want to do my room over, too! Mine's so babyish. Yours looks grown-up. Hey, what happened to your posters? Did your mom make you throw them out?"

Peichi smiled and got up to close her door. On the back of the door were two posters of Peichi's favorite bands. "I don't think Mom knows they're here!" she said, opening the door. Everybody laughed, and the girls made themselves comfortable on the big cushions.

Peichi sank into her big velvet chair. "*Aaaaahh!*" she sighed. "You guys have to try this!"

Amanda reached into her pocket. "Here's our money!" she said, waving a wad of bills. "I think Mrs. Jamison even put a tip in." She put the pile of cash on the floor.

"Money, money, money!" said Molly, throwing up a bunch of bills and watching them float to the floor. "I'll divide it up. One dollar for you, Peichi, one dollar for you, Amanda, one for Shawn, five dollars for me...," she joked.

"Maybe we should have a treasurer, like real clubs have," suggested Shawn. "Now that we have a real business, and we've made a little money."

"What does a treasurer do?" asked Molly.

"A treasurer takes care of all the money," Peichi explained.

"She writes down how much money comes in, divides it up, and keeps track of how it's spent," added Shawn.

Peichi looked around at her friends. "Can I do it?" she asked. "Or do you want to be the treasurer, Shawn?"

Shawn shook her head. "No, thanks," she said. She hadn't yet told Peichi that she would be leaving soon.

The girls looked at each other.

"Does anyone else want to be treasurer?" asked Molly. "Actually, I think I do. We'll have to take a vote."

"I'm definitely not voting for *you*, Molls," chuckled Amanda.

"Why not?" asked Molly with a pout.

Amanda giggled and told the friends, "One time Molly had a hole in her pocket and she lost all her allowance! And another time, she paid for an ice-cream cone with a ten-dollar bill and forgot to wait for her change, and the kid behind the counter had to chase her up the street to give it to her—"

"That was a long time ago, Manda," said Molly, rolling her eyes.

"If you call the beginning of the summer a long time ago," teased Amanda. She poked Molly in the ribs. "Plus, your money is always ending up in the wash."

"Well, at least it's clean!" Molly giggled. "Okay, so I won't be treasurer! Who wants Peichi to be treasurer?"

Everyone raised her hand.

"Then it's—what's that word?" asked Molly, handing the pile of bills over to Peichi. "When everyone votes for the same person?"

"Unanimous!" said Peichi. "Great! Thanks, guys! I'll

start right now!" She reached for a pad of paper. "Cooking job for the Jamisons..." She began to write. Then she took all the bills and divided the money equally among the friends.

"Hooray, I'm rich!" cried Molly. "Let's go to the movies! Let's buy some candy! Let's—"

"Hi, girls," called a gentle voice. The girls looked up. It was Mrs. Cheng, standing in the doorway. She looked like a model with her sleek black bobbed hair, flared jeans, and black sleeveless top.

"Oh, hi, Mom!" called Peichi. "You sneaked up on us."

"Moms are good at that," said Mrs. Cheng with a soft laugh. "You're all holding what looks like lots of money. Now don't spend it all in one place!"

"We won't," said Peichi. "Guess what? I'm treasurer of Dish!"

Mrs. Cheng came into the room and sat on the floor with the girls.

"Are you going to invest some money in Dish?" asked Mrs. Cheng. "I hope so."

"What does 'invest' mean?" asked Amanda.

Mrs. Cheng thought for a moment. "Well, it means to put some of the money you earned from Dish back *into* Dish. To buy things your business needs. For instance, I used some of the money I made from designing the logo for the Brooklyn Bank to buy a more powerful computer, and a better chair."

"We invested in the fridge, and it's paid off already," said Amanda. "Luckily, it was only forty-five dollars!"

"Great!" said Mrs. Cheng. "What does your business need now? Spices? Sugar? Flour?"

Molly and Amanda nodded as they looked at each other.

"We've just been using a lot of ingredients that Mom had," said Amanda.

"But we should buy our own stuff," added Molly, "so that Mom doesn't have to keep replacing what we take."

"And maybe we should buy your mom some supplies to pay her back for what we've already used," said Peichi.

Mrs. Cheng smiled. "You have the idea," she said.

"And we need to make flyers to advertise our business, and pay for an ad to put in the newspaper," Peichi added. "The ad will cost money."

"Maybe we don't even need an ad," said Shawn. "I mean, we're getting a lot of business already, and we might get more than we can handle."

Molly and Amanda flashed each other a look. Shawn was right. Once Shawn left, they'd be down to just themselves and Peichi.

Mrs. Cheng stood up to go. "I'll be happy to design a flyer if you girls want one," she offered. "And you don't have to pay me! Now come on down to the pool. It's too nice a day to be cooped up inside!"

"Okay," said the girls.

Peichi turned to her friends after Mrs. Cheng left. "We do need supplies. So, the best thing to do is for each of us to put back some of our money—let's say ten dollars. That'll give us forty dollars to start with."

Everyone gave Peichi ten dollars.

"Okay," she said. "I'll put this in an envelope and we'll take it shopping when we get our next job. And each time we get paid for a job, we should put in ten more dollars."

"Oh, well, I guess we're not rich anymore," said Molly.

"But we still have enough for an extra-large pizza and a movie tonight!" Peichi pointed out.

Molly and Amanda headed straight into the pool, but Shawn and Peichi sat at the little table near the pool and drank their sodas. That's when Shawn told Peichi that she would be leaving.

"Why?" exclaimed Peichi. "What about Dish? And all the fun we've been having? I wish—"

"It's just for a month," Shawn told her. It seemed like she'd said that a million times already.

"Oh, well," said Peichi with a shrug. "I'll miss you! I promise to send you lots of e-mails!"

"That would be great," said Shawn with a smile. "I'll miss you too."

Amanda stopped swimming and poked her head out

of the water. She saw Shawn smiling as she spoke to Peichi. Amanda knew she should try to see things Shawn's way, as Mom had said, but it really didn't seem like Shawn was going to miss them. Shawn looked too happy. *Way* too happy.

chapter 4

The next day was cooking class.

"Today's our last class," said Molly, when they met up with Shawn in her apartment building. "It's graduation day!"

"I wonder if Natasha will be in class?" asked Shawn.

Amanda sighed. "It's gonna be so weird if she is."

Natasha Ross was the most complicated person the girls knew. Last year she'd become the twins' and Shawn's first and only enemy. The girls still didn't know why Natasha had told the principal that they'd cheated on an important science test. The lie turned into a rumor that shot through the school, and there was nothing they could do to stop it.

The girls had decided to keep their distance from Natasha. But Natasha was impossible to avoid.

The girls ran into her *everywhere*, including cooking class. Mrs. Moore suspected that Natasha had an unhappy life. She encouraged the twins to forgive her and be as friendly as possible. So they were. Or at least they tried to be.

But it wasn't easy.

Then, suddenly, Natasha was calling them, wanting to

get together. The girls even went to a tea party at her house. And Natasha began to cook with them. The girls started to see another side of her—a shy, sweet side—and they began to trust her.

That's exactly when she ditched out of Dish, just as they were getting it off the ground. Suddenly, she was totally unreachable, and ignored them. At first the girls thought Natasha was just being difficult again, but then they found out what was really going on. It turned out that Natasha's dad had promised to lend the girls some money to help get Dish started.

Then he'd lost his job. He still wanted to give Natasha the money, but she felt guilty taking it. Too embarrassed to face her friends, she blew off helping them with a huge cooking job.

And the girls hadn't seen Natasha since.

Soon Molly, Amanda, and Shawn reached Park Terrace Cookware—the store where their cooking classes were held. They walked through the store to a large, gleaming kitchen in the back. In the center of the room were two rows of long tables with wooden tops and chrome legs. The tables held several workstations. Each student had his or her own cutting board and supplies. Today there was also a rolling pin—plus flour, salt, shortening, and milk, already measured. And there was a utensil that the girls didn't know what to do with.

Amanda looked around. No Natasha. So far, so good.

But Peichi was already there, talking nonstop to serious-looking David Stern. He couldn't seem to get a word in, so he just kept nodding his head. Then Peichi saw the girls.

"Hi!" Peichi ran over to the girls and greeted them. Her shiny black hair was up in a high ponytail, like the twins' hair. "What do you think the rolling pin's for? What do you think we're going to make today? I wonder if Natasha's gonna show up?"

Just then, Carmen Piccolo, the instructor, walked in and began to chat with some of the students. She wore her long reddish-blond hair in a ponytail. As she put on her chef's apron, the girls hurried to their workstations.

"Hello, class," said Carmen.

"Hi, Carmen!" chorused the class.

"Today is our last class," said Carmen. "You've all been so great. And as I promised in our first class, you're all getting graduation gifts. Freddie will pass them out!"

Just then, a young man with short dark hair and a goatee rushed in. Freddie Gonzalez was Carmen's assistant. He was *always* good for a laugh.

He began to hand out a chef's apron and an instant camera to each student. "How ya doin' today, Connor?...

Looking good, Omar, looking good!... What's up, Peichi?"

"Look!" said Peichi, holding up her apron. "It has my name embroidered on it! And they even spelled it right!"

Everyone checked out their names on their aprons. Under their names, PARK TERRACE COOKWARE was embroidered in smaller letters.

"Cool!" lots of kids were saying as they put on their aprons.

"I'm a professional now," said Omar, striking a pose. "Now all I need is a tall white chef's hat."

"Actually, that's called a *toque blanche,*" said David, as he pushed up his glasses.

"I'm glad you like your aprons," said Carmen. "Today is our pie workshop! We're going to learn how to make piecrust!"

"Piecrust?" protested some of the boys.

"Yeah, piecrust, man!" said Freddie. "Come on, Connor, you know you love pie. You, too, Omar. Now you'll be able to make a pie whenever you want, and it'll taste better than your momma's."

"You mean we're not going to make a whole meal, like we usually do?" asked Peichi.

"That's right," replied Carmen. "Piecrusts take time to

make, especially when you've never made one before. Today we're going to make chocolate cream pie. That has just one crust—the bottom crust. That's enough for today."

"*Mmmm*, chocolate cream pie," said Amanda dreamily to herself. But most of the kids heard her, and laughed. Amanda blushed deep red and pretended to be fascinated with her rolling pin.

"Each of you will make your own pastry dough," Carmen went on. "We'll use a few of these pastry shells for today's pies, and the rest of you can take yours home. Let's get started! To save time, Freddie has already measured out the ingredients for the crust."

As she always did, Carmen stood at the front of the class so she could demonstrate everything the students were supposed to do.

"I'm going to tell you something my mom told me the first time we made a pie together," announced Carmen. "'Don't be afraid of the dough!' Remember—you're the boss, not the pie dough."

The class chuckled.

"If you remember that, you'll have more fun," Carmen went on. "Okay. First let's mix the salt and flour together in your mixing bowl." Everyone followed along. Then Carmen picked up the strange-looking round utensil that had a handle attached to strips of curved metal.

"This is called a pastry cutter, or pastry blender," she told the class. "Watch me use it to cut the shortening through the flour."

Carmen added the shortening, then pressed the pastry cutter down into the ingredients. The metal strips helped combine the ingredients. "Now you try," she said. "Do it until your shortening looks like giant peas."

"This is hard," complained Connor after a while. "My dough keeps sticking to the pastry cutter." The class giggled, because every week, Connor said exactly what most of them were thinking.

"This is nothin'," cracked Omar. "You're just lazy." Connor and Omar were always goofing on each other.

"You can scrape off the dough with a butter knife," Carmen told Connor. "Freddie will bring you one." She addressed the class again. "This takes patience," said Carmen. "When you bake—especially pastry—you always need to be patient."

After that, the class followed Carmen as she sprinkled milk on the flour and mixed it lightly with a fork until all the flour was moistened and stuck together.

Next Carmen gathered the dough

together with her hands, and pressed it firmly into a ball.

"Yo, watch it. This isn't pizza dough," warned Freddie, when some of the boys pretended to throw their balls of dough up in the air.

The girls in the class rolled their eyes at one another. The boys were always acting up, and in almost every class they eventually had to be separated.

"Now we'll wrap the dough in wax paper and chill it," said Carmen. "Just like you guys in the corner need to chill!" she joked.

"Why do we need to chill the dough?" asked Peichi.

"If you didn't chill the dough, it would be too sticky to work with," replied Carmen. "Which would force you to add more flour. Then the baked piecrust would be tough, not crumbly. This dough should chill for about two hours. But we don't have that much time in class, so we'll have to put it in the freezer and just get it as cold as we can, while we make the chocolate filling."

Carmen broke the class into groups to make the filling. The students counted off in threes. Molly and Peichi ended up with Connor and Omar.

"Oh, no! Not her!" Omar said. He was talking about Peichi, whose constant chatter drove him nuts.

"You're so lucky you're with us," boasted Peichi. "'Cause *we* are gonna show you how to do it right."

"I've made pies before," said Omar. "Lots of 'em."

"Yeah, right," said Molly, not looking up from the recipe. She handed Omar a measuring cup. "Here. Measure a cup and a half of sugar."

"Okay," Omar said.

Molly cut up some squares of unsweetened chocolate, and Peichi separated some eggs, then gently beat the yolks with a fork. Omar stirred three cups of milk into a mixture of sugar, salt, flour, and cornstarch, added in the pieces of the chocolate, and cooked it over medium heat.

Freddie came running over. "You have to stir it constantly!" he said. "Good job."

"Wow, this smells great already!" said Peichi. "It's like chocolate pudding!"

The mixture began to thicken as it boiled. Omar let it boil for one minute, took it off the heat, and slowly stirred half the mixture into the egg yolks.

"Okay, now we pour this mixture back into the pan," read Molly, "and boil it for another minute."

After the mixture boiled, Omar took the pan off the heat, and Connor blended in some butter and vanilla. "Wow, that's rich," he said. "Now we chill it in the fridge."

Just about everyone in the class thought that making piecrust was difficult, but fun. The kids learned to dampen their work surface and put down a large piece of waxed paper, then spread the chilled dough by hand on the paper. They topped the dough with another piece of waxed paper, and rolled out the dough with their rolling pins.

"Yo, not too hard," Freddie told Omar. "Now keep turning the whole thing. Excellent, my man! You're almost home!"

Once the kids had rolled out their dough to fit the pie pan—with enough to lap over the sides—they removed the waxed paper from the top of the dough and laid the dough down in the pan. It was time to remove the other piece of waxed paper by starting on one side, and carefully rolling it toward themselves.

The fun part was to fit the dough into the pan. If it tore, the kids just patched it. Then they trimmed the dough with a knife all around the pan, turned it under, and crimped it with their fingers.

Carmen and Freddie took one last walk around the class to help the students.

"Your pastry shells really look great," Carmen announced. "I'm impressed! Now we're ready to bake them."

While the pies baked, the kids helped clean up. And they posed for pictures with their classmates.

"I'm gonna miss everyone!" said Peichi. "Oh, this is so sad!"

"You'll forget how sad you are when we eat those pies," said Omar.

Eight minutes later, as the students began to take their pastry shells out of the oven, the class got noisy.

"Wow! It's nice and brown."

"This looks awesome!"

"Man, I'm *good* at this!"

"*Aww*, mine's bad."

"No, it isn't. Just a little higher on one side."

Now it was time to pour the chilled chocolate filling into the shells.

"To finish the pies, we'll just add dollops of whipped cream," said Carmen.

"What are dollops?" asked Peichi.

"Globs," said Freddie. "Here's a dollop on your nose!" He topped off Peichi's nose with whipped cream.

Later, at the big table with china dessert plates and a white linen tablecloth, the class agreed that they'd never tasted anything so good.

"I can't believe we made this!" exclaimed Peichi.

Everyone traded e-mail addresses and laughed and ate.

Soon it was time to leave.

"We'll miss you," Molly said to Carmen and Freddie.

"Ah! You'll see me around the neighborhood," said Freddie. "I just got a job at Luigi's Restaurant."

"I loved having you girls in my class," said Carmen. "Good luck with your cooking business!" The girls had told Carmen about Dish, and she thought it was a great idea.

"Bye!" called Carmen as the students began to leave. "Don't forget to sign up for my gingerbread-house workshop in December!"

As they walked home, the girls talked about how much they had enjoyed their cooking classes.

"The best thing we made was when we carved the peacocks out of melons," Shawn said.

"No way—those chocolate cream pies were definitely my favorite!" replied Amanda.

"Yeah, we all know why that is!" Molly joked. Amanda's sweet tooth was intense.

"It's so hot!" Peichi complained. "Let's go somewhere with air conditioning. I know! Let's go to the movies! We still have that money from our last cooking job. We could just sit in the theater for a couple of hours and chill. What do you guys think?"

"Yeah, let's do that!" Molly cried.

"I can't," said Shawn, looking at her watch. "I have to get home and finish packing."

"Oh, okay," Amanda said, trying not to sound disappointed. "Well, why don't you call us after you finish packing? We can do something then."

"Um, I really don't think I can," Shawn said, looking uncomfortable. "My dad and I are having a special dinner tonight. After tomorrow, I'm not going to see him for a whole month."

You're not going to see us for a whole month, either, Amanda thought, but she didn't say anything.

"But let's get together tomorrow afternoon instead. Are you guys free? We could go out to lunch or something," Shawn continued.

"That sounds great! We can go to Harry's," Peichi said with a big smile.

But no one else looked very happy.

chapter 5

"*Mmm*—I'm gonna mi*th thith*," said Shawn thickly through a big bite of a double-chocolate brownie the day after class.

The friends were having a farewell snack at Harry's, their favorite hangout in Park Terrace. Harry's was an old pharmacy that had been turned into a funky coffeehouse. The girls loved hanging out there. Most everyone else their age was still hanging out in fast-food places with bright lights, screaming kids, and greasy burgers or pizza. But they were eating veggie wraps and poppy-seed cake on round marble-topped tables, surrounded by writers, artists, and college students. It made them feel older.

"What time is your flight?" asked Peichi. "Are you all packed? Are you taking a lot of stuff?"

"My flight's at seven," replied Shawn. "Well, you guys, I should get going. I'm all packed, but I want to spend the rest of the day with my dad."

"Okay," said all the girls at once. They quickly

finished up their wraps and brownies, then walked Shawn back to the lobby of her apartment building.

"Have a good time," Molly told Shawn, remembering not to act sad.

Shawn smiled. "Thanks," she said. "Have a great month. I'll send you lots of e-mails, and you'd better write me back!"

"Don't worry, we will," Amanda assured Shawn. "Every day."

They waited in silence for the elevator to come. Amanda really wanted to give Shawn a good-bye hug, but Shawn looked pretty uncomfortable.

The elevator door opened, and Shawn got in.

"We'll miss you!" said Peichi. "Bye!"

"Bye, Shawn," said the twins at the same time. They gave Shawn a little wave.

"Bye, you guys! I'll see you in a month."

Shawn waved until the door closed.

"What are you two doing now?" asked Peichi, as the girls walked away from Shawn's building.

"Nothing much," said Molly gloomily.

"We both have to practice the piano this afternoon," Amanda reminded Molly.

"Hey, I have an idea!" exclaimed Peichi. "Let's all go to Chinatown, and surprise my grandparents at their store!"

"You mean right now? On the subway?" asked Amanda. Peichi's grandparents' store was in Manhattan, across the river from Brooklyn.

"Yeah! It doesn't take long to get there," replied Peichi.

"We're not allowed to ride the subway by ourselves," said Amanda. "Are you?"

"No," admitted Peichi. "But if we all go together, I think it would be okay. Come on! Let's do it. The subway's just a block from here. We could be there in half an hour, maybe less!"

"No, we can't," said Amanda firmly.

"I'll go!" Molly blurted out. "I feel like doing something different."

Amanda's eyes widened. "What!" she cried, looking at Molly.

"We'll be with Peichi's grandparents," Molly told her. "It's no big deal."

"Well, I'm not going," said Amanda.

"Okay," said Molly. "But I am."

Amanda's mouth dropped open. What was with them?

"Well, here we are," said Peichi, pointing at the subway entrance. "We'll be back in a few hours! No one will even know we were there."

Suddenly Amanda felt all alone.

"Sure you don't want to come?" Molly asked her.

Amanda shrugged. "Have fun," she said. That was her answer.

"Okay, then, bye," said Molly.

"Byeeee!" said Peichi brightly. "Oh, I hear the train!" And she and Molly turned and hurried, giggling, down the steps and out of sight.

Amanda didn't move for a while. She just stood and stared down the subway steps. Then she walked home with a lump in her throat.

Peichi and Molly ran down two flights of stairs. They heard a deep rumbling sound getting louder and louder, and felt a *whoosh* of cool air on their faces. The train was coming.

"Hurry!" cried Peichi. "We still have to buy our MetroCards!"

At the MetroCard machine, the girls giggled nervously as they quickly searched their pockets for money.

The train roared into the station just as Molly and Peichi got their cards. They cranked through the turnstiles and got on the train. The doors closed behind them, and they were on their way.

"This was a great idea!" exclaimed Molly, trying to catch her breath.

Peichi was right. Less than half an hour later, the train got to Canal Street.

"This is it!" cried Peichi. The girls hurried off the train and up the stairs, into bright sunlight and bustling Chinatown.

"Okay," said Peichi, looking around. "I know exactly where we are. All we have to do is go down Canal Street and find Mulberry Street. This way!" She led Molly through the congested street. "Have you ever been to Chinatown before?"

"Just once, for dinner, and that was at night. Look at all these store signs in Chinese! Can you read them?"

"Not really," admitted Peichi. "But I'm learning."

"Whoa," said Molly, as the smell of fresh fish hit her. The girls had come to an open-air fish stand covered with an awning. It led to an indoor fish market. "Oooh! What are these big fish with the whiskers? They're still alive!"

"Those are catfish," said Peichi. "Yum! Look—live lobsters, too. I love lobster."

Street vendors sold all kinds of stuff right on the sidewalks. Bamboo. Pocketbooks. Electronics. Socks. Dragon and Buddha sculptures. Vegetables, some of which Molly had never seen.

"You can buy anything in Chinatown," observed Molly. "But it's so crowded here! It's hard to walk around." She heard Chinese being spoken all around her, mixed in with accents and other foreign languages. It seemed to Molly like the whole world had come to Chinatown that day.

Peichi suddenly stopped walking. "*Hmmm*," she murmured, looking up and around. "I don't remember this bakery."

"What's the matter?" asked Molly.

Peichi frowned. "Uh, we should have come to Mulberry by now."

"You mean, we're lost?" asked Molly. The sun was beating down on her face. She wished she had her sunglasses. Throngs of tourists and shoppers threatened to separate her from Peichi.

"Oh! I know," said Peichi. "We went the wrong way down Canal. Let's turn around."

Whatever, thought Molly. *Just as long as we're not lost*. Someone bumped into her. Suddenly she felt like she was a million miles from home.

The girls turned back and finally came to Mulberry Street. They turned right, and came upon a store with a big awning. Rows and rows of cooked ducks hung displayed in the window.

"This is it!" cried Peichi. "It's one of the biggest stores in Chinatown. You'll see."

The girls went inside. A long line of people waited patiently for a duck, crispy chicken, or barbecued spareribs. But that part of the store was small and almost separate from the rest of it.

Peichi spotted her grandfather filling a large jar with loose tea leaves. "Hi, Ah-yeh!" she called, going toward him.

Startled, the senior Mr. Cheng turned around.

"Peichi!" he cried in surprise. He hugged her and said some words to her in Chinese. Then he saw Molly. "Hello," he said, nodding and smiling.

"Ah-yeh, this is my friend Molly," said Peichi. "Molly, this is my grandfather."

"Hello, Mr. Cheng," said Molly, blushing. She always felt awkward around adults she didn't know.

Peichi's grandfather called out something in Chinese, and Peichi's grandmother appeared from a back room.

"Peichi!"

"Surprise, Ah-mah!" cried Peichi, reaching out for a hug. Then she introduced Molly.

While Peichi was busy talking to her grandparents, Molly decided to explore. She was staring at a display of shredded squid when Peichi caught up to her. "Come on, I'll show you around," she said to Molly.

The girls wandered up and down the aisles. Molly hardly recognized any of the food for sale.

"This is one of my favorite snacks," Peichi said, holding up a foil package. "Roasted hot green peas. And here are shrimp chips!"

They came to the tea section, where lots of people were reaching for pretty tins of all kinds of teas. There were big jars of tea leaves. And there were porcelain tea sets and rice bowls.

And then there was the sweets aisle.

Molly picked up a clear package of round, striped cookies. "Umbrella cookies," she read. Not every package was printed in Chinese.

Peichi picked up a package of candies that were wrapped in red foil. "These candies are so good! They're strawberry flavored. We always eat them during Chinese New Year." Suddenly the package slipped from Peichi's hand and fell to the floor. "Whoops," she said, and kneeled down to pick it up.

Peichi didn't get up right away.

"What are you doing?" asked Molly. "We really need to get going." She was getting nervous about the time.

"There's something under this shelf," said Peichi. "*Oof.*" She grunted as she reached her arm as far as it would go. "Here it is."

Peichi had found a small pouch. "There's something in it!" she said in a loud whisper.

"What is it?" asked Molly. "Open it!"

"I'm trying to," said Peichi. "It's hard to open." Inside the pouch was a package that was taped shut.

"*Ohmygosh!*" exclaimed the girls as Peichi finally unwrapped a large grayish, yellow-green gemstone. It was a disc-shaped pendant, highly polished with a beautiful carving of a dragon and elaborate designs.

"This is jade!" said Peichi.

"Jade?" asked Molly. "I've never seen this stone before."

"Jade is used a lot in China," said Peichi. "And guess what? 'Peichi' means 'precious jade'. This couldn't be real, though. It's too big. But it's so pretty! Cool!" She stuffed the pendant in the pocket of her denim skirt.

"Uh, Peichi, aren't you going to show it to your grandma?" asked Molly, frowning.

"Sure," replied Peichi breezily. "But see how busy she is? She and Ah-yeh are coming over next weekend. I'll show her then. I just want to hold on to it for a couple of days."

"But what if it's *really* real?" Molly said. "What if someone lost it, and has been looking all over for it?"

"I doubt it," Peichi said. "About the real part. I mean, do you know how much this would be worth if it were real? A *lot* of money!"

"Well, it *could* be real," Molly said.

Peichi took the stone out of her pocket and looked at it. What if Molly was right?

"I really think you should show it to your grand-mother," Molly repeated.

Peichi looked over at Ah-mah. She was still busy with customers. "Well, I don't want to bother her now. She looks busy," Peichi told Molly. "I promise I'll show it to her next week. Besides, if it were really real, someone would have put up a lost sign, don't you think?"

Molly shrugged. "I'm not sure. But I'll tell you what I am sure of—we have to get going!" It seemed as if they'd been gone from home a long time.

"Okay," said Peichi. They waved good-bye to her grandparents, and headed to the subway.

The girls were lucky again. The train was just heading into the station when they got downstairs.

"*Whew,*" said Molly. "No waiting, what a relief."

But that's when their luck ran out.

On the subway car, Peichi suddenly saw a familiar head of hair behind a newspaper, and her stomach churned. *Her dad was standing two feet away from them!* He was coming home from work.

Peichi motioned to Molly to walk the other way, but the car was so crowded that Molly couldn't get through. Turning the page of his newspaper, Mr. Cheng suddenly saw the girls.

"Peichi! Molly!" he said, surprised. "What are you girls doing here?"

chapter 6

While Molly and Peichi were having their Chinatown adventure, Amanda was practicing a difficult new piece of music. As her fingers fumbled over wrong notes, she wondered what her sister and Peichi were up to. Neither of them ever broke rules, so what was up with them now? Amanda banged her hands on the keys. Kitty let out a loud *meow* and scampered away. *Maybe I should have gone, too,* Amanda thought. *They're probably having a blast!*

BRRRIIING! Amanda jumped off the piano bench and ran to the phone.

"Hello?" she said.

"Is this the Moore residence?" asked a high-pitched woman's voice.

"Yes."

"This is Ms. Brenda Barlow," stated the caller. "With whom am I speaking?"

"I'm Amanda Moore."

"I'm calling about the cooking service, dear. I got your name from Ella Jamison. She's a *very* good friend of mine, and she just *raved* about what good little *cooks* you are!"

"Oh," said Amanda. "That's—that's nice. Thank you. I mean, please tell her thank you."

"I certainly *will*, my dear. And *I'd* like to hire you to do just one little dinner for me. It's next weekend. It's my little angel's birthday, and I'm having her aunt and uncle over, and her grandmother. I'm actually a *terrific* cook, but I'm just *terribly* busy, and won't be able to do it myself. I'd like something simple, just a roasted chicken, a nice salad, *that* sort of thing. Can you do that?"

"Sure," said Amanda. "We can definitely make that."

"Naturally, dear, I'll need some desserts, too."

Amanda felt her face get hot. "Well, I don't know if we could do a birthday cake. We haven't made a layer cake before—"

"No need for a birthday cake, dear. No need at *all*. My little angel would rather have cupcakes anyway. You *do*

make cupcakes, don't you? Young girls still *love* to make cupcakes, don't they?"

Amanda pretended to cough to hide a laugh. This woman was too much! "We could make cupcakes," she replied. "And even a fruit cobbler if you want something besides cupcakes."

"How much will all this cost?" Ms. Barlow asked.

"I-I'll have to get back to you," Amanda told her. There was no way she was going to set a price without talking to the other girls first.

"Okay," Ms. Barlow replied. "Well, whatever it is, I'm sure it'll be just fine! It all sounds *perfect.* I live at one twenty-four Carroll Place. Please deliver the food at four o'clock on Saturday. Good-bye."

"Good-bye," said Amanda, but Ms. Brenda Barlow had already hung up.

Five minutes later, the phone rang again. It was Mrs. Jamison, telling her that her neighbor, Brenda Barlow, might call to place an order. Also, Mrs. Jamison wanted to know if the girls could cook up three days' worth of dinners and deliver them in two days. Mrs. Jamison was going to have knee surgery and wanted to have food in the house. Amanda accepted the job, thanked Mrs. Jamison, and hung up.

That's when the phone rang for the third time.

"Hello?"

"Dear, it's Ms. Brenda Barlow again. *Listen,*" said the woman breathlessly, "I know I said *next* weekend, but something *very* important has come up for next weekend, and now I need to schedule this dinner for two nights from now."

"Oh, I'm sorry, Ms. Barlow, but we'll be too busy cooking for Mrs. Jamison that day."

There was a pause.

"Well, I'm just *desperate* for you to do it. Please!

You *can't* back out now! That wouldn't be right, my dear. You *already* made a commitment!"

Amanda didn't know what to say. This lady is whacked, she thought. She's the one who changed the dates! I'm NOT going to give in to her! But Amanda's tongue felt too big in her mouth when she tried to say "no" again. She'd never had to argue with an adult before—at least, not with one she didn't know! So she finally said, "Okay," just to get rid of Ms. Barlow. Hanging up the phone, Amanda thought, *Well, Mom is just going to have to help us with all this cooking.*

That's exactly when Mom got home from work. She taught art history at Brooklyn University.

"Hi, sweetie, do you want some lemonade? Where's Molly?" she asked.

"Uh. She's at—she's with—I mean, she and Peichi are swimming. You know, at her house. I just wanted to—stay home."

"Oh," said Mom. "Why did you want to stay home, honey? Don't you feel well?"

"Well, no. I mean, yes, I feel fine. I don't know, I guess I just wanted to practice a lot today," said Amanda lamely. She shrugged and tried to look casual. Amanda was a terrible liar. And she was also getting a sinking feeling about all the work Dish would soon have, without Shawn's help.

"Okay," said Mom, but she looked concerned. "Well, I'm going to change my clothes. When you're finished practicing, come out to the garden."

Later, in the garden with Mom, Amanda pretended to be deep in a book so that she wouldn't have to say much. She felt like anything she said would give away Molly's secret. *Where is she?* Amanda began to wonder, as the afternoon wore on.

Finally, Molly's face appeared at the screen door that led to the garden. She looked pretty gloomy—not like someone who'd just had an amazing adventure.

"Hi, Molls!" said Mom.

Molly didn't say anything right away. But Amanda could tell that Molly took a deep breath before she opened the screen door.

"Hi, Mom," Molly said, stepping outside.

"Did you swim?"

"Swim?"

"Um, I told Mom you were at Peichi's," said Amanda quickly.

"No. I wasn't at Peichi's."

Mom looked surprised. Then she smiled. "Then where were you, sweetie?"

"Peichi and I went to Chinatown. On the subway. By ourselves. Even though we knew we weren't supposed to. And then we ran into Mr. Cheng on the subway, on the way home."

"Molly!" cried Mom. Then she turned to Amanda. "Amanda! You lied to me!"

The twins looked down at the ground.

"Well, I don't know what to say," began Mom. She was still shocked.

Then she got mad.

"Yes, I *do* know what to say! Molly, you thought you were going to have big fun, didn't you! And no one was going to find out. Well, what you did was very dangerous. And very irresponsible. And Amanda, I'm surprised at you, too. It's not like you to lie like that."

"Well, at least I didn't go with them," said Amanda meekly.

Mom didn't even hear her. Her eyes bore down on Molly.

"Amelia, you're grounded for a week," stated Mom.

Amelia! Whoa! She never calls me that, thought Molly. Amelia was her real name.

"...And that means no computer time, either," Mom went on. "Amanda, you're off the computer, too. And you can forget about your little shopping trips and our outings to the nail salon for a while." Lately, Amanda and Mom had enjoyed getting manicures together at a neighborhood salon.

"I'm sorry, Mom," said Molly, fighting back tears. "I really am."

"Me, too, Mom," said Amanda. "I'll never lie to you again."

Then the worst thing happened.

Mom looked sadly at the twins and said softly, "I trusted you girls." She coolly walked into the house as Molly jumped out of her way.

Now the twins were alone in the garden. Usually they loved hanging out there. The garden was long and narrow, made private by a high wooden fence. A one-hundred-year-old tree provided lots of shade. Colorful flowers, a picnic table, and lawn chairs made it the perfect summer hangout. But right now the garden just seemed lonely.

"Oh! This is such a drag," moaned Molly. "Mom's never gonna trust me again."

"All you think about is yourself!" snapped Amanda. "Look at me. I'm in trouble, too. Because I lied for you."

"Well," countered Molly, "you didn't have to lie for me."

"Didn't—didn't *have* to!" sputtered Amanda. "Well, don't worry—I never will again. But now I'm really in trouble. Because we got two cooking jobs today while you and Peichi were running around Chinatown. And I'll bet Peichi gets grounded, too, so we've lost her, and we've lost Shawn, and guess what? We have to do it all. And there's no way Mom will help us now." She folded her arms over her chest and stormed out of the garden, leaving Molly all by herself.

Molly and Amanda weren't able to go online. Shawn, of course, didn't know that.

To: mooretimes2
From: Ruth Jordan
Date: 7/18, 9:45 PM
Re: I'm here

Hi, guys!
My flight was good. They gave me extra nuts and I didn't even have to ask this time. But a lady next to me FLOSSED HER TEETH, in her seat! Can you even believe how gross that was?????
Anyway, Grandma Ruthie and Sonia and Jamal all met me at the airport. It's

good to be here. What did you guys
do today? Write me back soon, and put
"For Shawn" in the "Re:" box so G.
Ruthie knows it's 4 me.
    xox Shawn

"**M**om, can you please help us?" asked Amanda late that night. "I'm really sorry for lying to you. But now we have all this work, and I have no idea how we'll get it done. Peichi is grounded, too, and Shawn's gone."

"Sorry, Amanda, but I think you will have to work this out on your own," replied Mom. "You should never assume that I can help you. You know I love to cook with you girls every chance I can get, but you need to ask me first. I'm very busy with my own work right now. Dish is your business, and you need to learn what the responsibilities of having a business are all about."

"Yeah, I know, but I didn't think Molly and Peichi would be grounded."

"That's what I'm talking about," said Mom firmly. "If you're going to have a business, you all have to behave in a way that won't hurt your business."

Amanda sighed. Deep down, she knew Mom was right.

The next morning, as Molly practiced the piano, Amanda took her parents' work clothes to the dry cleaner's down the street. She did it as a favor to Mom, to try to get back on her good side. Plus, she really needed to go outside. At least she was allowed to get out of the house—unlike Molly!

As she walked home, she daydreamed about what she could say to get out of the two cooking jobs.

I'm sorry, Mrs. Jamison, I'm sorry, Ms. Barlow, but something terrible happened. We're all in the hospital. For food poisoning! From something we cooked! Right, so you wouldn't want us to cook for you anyway...

Suddenly, up the street, Amanda saw a familiar-looking ball cap.

Justin McElroy's ball cap.

Justin was the new kid on Taft Street. The McElroys had recently moved to New York from Chicago. Justin was eleven, the same age as the girls. While Molly and Peichi thought he was no different from any other neighborhood kid, Amanda and Shawn thought he was pretty cute with his gelled reddish-brown hair and deep brown eyes. Like Peichi, he was the kind of person who always looked happy, even when he wasn't smiling.

Earlier in the summer, a small electrical fire had ruined the McElroy's kitchen. The McElroys had had to leave the house they'd just moved into so that the contractor could renovate the kitchen. Peichi's parents had let them rent an apartment they owned nearby on Garden Street. And it was Mrs. Moore's great idea to cook up a week's supply of dinners for the McElroys, to help them out during that difficult time.

The girls had just started their cooking classes and formed their own weekly cooking club. They had had a blast cooking together with Mrs. Moore, and loved knowing that they'd been a big help to the McElroys. Then, they cooked a ton of food for Mrs. Moore's surprise birthday party.

All that cooking gave Mrs. Moore another idea. She hired the girls to cook a week's supply of dinners, since she was heading off on a long business trip. And Mrs. McElroy had told a neighbor about the girls and their cooking, which led to their second job.

Now they had Dish, their own business. It had all happened so fast—too fast. And while they were gaining jobs, they'd already lost two members—Natasha and Shawn. At least for now. And Peichi, sort of.

"Hi, Justin," called Amanda.

Justin turned around. "Hi," he said uncertainly.

"It's Amanda," said Amanda with a laugh.

"Right!" said Justin. He grinned. "Sorry. I can't tell you and Molly apart yet."

"So, are you all moved back into your house?" asked Amanda.

"Yeah, we're back in. It feels good."

"Great!" said Amanda.

There was an uncomfortable pause.

"So," Amanda added casually, "what are you up to today?"

Justin shrugged. "Nothing much," he said. "It seems like all the guys I know are on vacation. There's not much to do."

Ding! A thought popped into Amanda's head. "How would you like to make some money helping us cook?" she blurted out.

She almost gasped. Had she just asked Justin to cook with them?

"Cook with you?" asked Justin, surprised.

For a moment, Amanda thought he was making fun of her, and she wanted to disappear.

"Well," said Amanda. She wanted to take it all back. Instead, she said, "It's just that you told us once, when we ran into you at the supermarket, that you like to cook." She quickly told him about Dish, and how they were down to just two cooks.

"Sure, why not?" replied Justin. "You guys helped my family. I owe ya one!"

Meanwhile, Peichi was in her room, moping about the trouble she'd gotten into.

"You've always been respectful of our rules," her parents had said to her. "What made you do something like this?"

She sat on her bed and pulled the jade pendant out of its pouch. She put it on an old chain, tried it on, and modeled it in the mirror.

But it didn't feel good to wear it.

She took it off, put it back in the pouch, and hid it in a drawer in her new desk. She wasn't going to tell her parents she'd found it.

Not yet.

She'd probably just get into trouble again.

To: mooretimes2, happyface
From: Ruth Jordan
Date: 7/20, 4:53 PM
Re: What's up?

Hey Molly and Amanda and Peichi!
    What's going on with the Chef Girls? Are you guys too busy in the kitchen to e-mail me? j/k! Have you tried any new recipes? Is Dish

still getting lots of new customers?

I am sooo tired. Last night I slept over at Sonia's. We had the best time! We gave each other pedicures and then she gave me some of this mint facial mask. It made my skin all tingly and glow-y and it felt really cool. I will definitely bring back some for u to try! Then we stayed up really late watching movies we rented. I slept through lunch today!

Tomorrow we're having a family picnic at the beach. Everybody's making something different and I think I wanna bring that potato salad u made for your mom's birthday party. Can u e-mail me the recipe please? I miss you guys a lot! E-mail me SOON and fill me in on what's up!

xox
Shawn

8

"**M**rs. Tortelli called," Molly told Amanda when Amanda got home from the dry cleaner's. "She's sick, and she asked if we would walk Casey." Casey was her cute dog, a little beagle.

"Well, I guess that means me," said Amanda.

"I wish I could go, too," said Molly. "Are you going to take Casey to the dog run at the park?"

"Uh-huh," said Amanda in a faraway voice.

"What's up?" asked Molly. "What are you thinking about?"

"Oh," said Amanda. "Well, I ran into Justin. And I asked him if he'd help us cook for these two jobs. And— he actually said yes!"

"What!" cried Molly. "I can't believe you asked him!"

"I can't believe he said yes," murmured Amanda.

"But," protested Molly, "we don't even know Justin. I don't want a boy in our group. It'll be weird having him here."

"It'll be better than *not* having him here," retorted Amanda. "We need him! And it's just this once. He won't be a permanent member of Dish."

Molly didn't say anything. She was too busy sulking.

Amanda didn't really care. She had enough to worry about, like all the food they had to cook. *And I hope I don't do anything stupid around Justin,* she thought, *like a few weeks ago when I tripped and fell on my face, right in front of him and all of his friends!*

"C'mon, Casey, we're going to the dog run!" cried Amanda an hour later, as she jogged up the hill to the park. Casey trotted beside her.

There were only a few people at the dog run—a lady with her poodle, a group of teenagers watching a yellow lab play, a tall blond girl with her terrier...

Oh, no! thought Amanda. The girl was Natasha.

It was too late to leave the dog run. Natasha had spotted Amanda at the same time.

Amanda waved limply, and Natasha eventually came over, with her dog, Willy, trotting behind her.

Luckily, the dogs helped break the ice. Amanda reached down to give Willy a pat as Natasha said, "Hi, Amanda, who's this? Down, Willy!"

"This is Casey, our neighbor's dog. Say hi to Willy, Casey."

Natasha and Amanda watched the dogs greet each other.

It was time for someone to say something.

"So, what's new?" asked Amanda. "We missed you in class. We made pies and graduated and got chef's aprons with our names on them."

"I know. Carmen called me to tell me they're holding my apron for me at the store. I just got back from Cape Cod. Uh—how is everyone?"

Amanda cleared her throat. Should she tell Natasha everything? She didn't want to be too chatty, as if nothing had gone wrong between them. But she said, "Well, Shawn's dad had to go to Australia and New Zealand, so she went back down to South Carolina."

"Really!"

"Yeah, and Peichi and Molly are grounded right now—"

"Wow! Why?"

"—and Dish got two more cooking jobs, and I'll have to do a lot of the work. Luckily, Justin's going to help us out."

Natasha's cold blue eyes widened. "Justin *McElroy?* Wow!"

"Uh-huh," said Amanda, trying to sound casual.

Natasha stuffed her free hand into her cutoff shorts, something she always did when she was nervous. "Well," she said, "if you need another cook, you know, uh, I could help you."

Yeah, right! Amanda thought. *There's no way I'm trusting this girl again!*

Amanda bent down to pet Casey.

She glanced back up and saw Natasha's eyes, looking anxious.

Sad.

That's why Amanda heard herself saying, "Sure, that would be great. Can you come over tomorrow morning?"

Oh my gosh! Amanda thought. *What did I just say?!*

Natasha brightened. "Yeah! I'll be there!"

Suddenly, Amanda felt relieved. With four cooks, they could definitely handle all the work. And things wouldn't be so awkward with Justin if another person was there, too.

"Great. Thanks."

Natasha checked her watch. "*Oops,* I have to go to the dentist soon," she said. "I'll see you tomorrow!" She turned to leave, and then stopped. "Amanda?"

"Yes?"

"I'm sorry about...everything. Not showing up to help you that time. Dropping out of Dish without telling you. All that stuff. I—I did everything wrong. And I've—I've missed you guys."

"It's okay, Natasha. See you tomorrow."

Amanda dropped Casey off at the Tortellis' and found Molly in the garden.

"Where's Matthew?" asked Amanda as she flopped into a chair.

"Soccer practice."

"Well," said Amanda, "you'll never believe what just happened. This day has been so weird!"

"What happened?" asked Molly.

"I ran into Natasha. With Willy at the dog run. She just got back from Cape Cod. She was tan."

"Really."

"And she asked if she could help us tomorrow."

"Wow!"

"And she said she was sorry about everything."

"*Hmm.*" Molly tried to picture all of this. "What did you say?"

"I said, 'okay.'"

Molly rolled her eyes. "Let's see, today is Wednesday, so Natasha's our friend again—"

"Molly, we're desperate! We've got two huge jobs that are really stressing me out! Why aren't you freaking?"

"She'd better just show up, then."

"I know. But what if she doesn't? It'll be such a mess."

"Is she going with you to the store?" asked Molly.

Amanda slapped her forehead. "Oh, I forgot! How am

I going to do all this shopping by myself? I really should go now."

"Call her."

"No, she's at the dentist," said Amanda irritably. She sighed. "You're right, what if she doesn't show up? She's done that before when we needed her. And now I have to go to the store. I need to buy so much stuff that I'll have to make more than one trip. Why did you have to go and get grounded?"

Molly suddenly looked embarrassed. "I'm sorry, Manda."

Then the twins looked at each other. They were having the "twin thing." And it was a rather wicked thought this time.

"No," Amanda told Molly. She giggled.

"You're right, I shouldn't go to the store with you, even though no one would know," said Molly. "Nobody would find out, right? Mom's at work for two more hours..."

"Better not do it," said Amanda. "We're in enough trouble as it is. No, I'll just go by myself, and lug all those heavy bags home." She sighed heavily.

Molly and Amanda missed another e-mail from Shawn.

Wuzzup with u? Did u forget how to turn on the computer?

Yesterday I went to Myrtle Beach for our family picnic. It was so great! I used Grandma Ruthie's potato salad recipe since I didn't get one from you.

I'm getting better at bodysurfing but I still got pretty pounded! Are you cooking? Swimming at Peichi's? Going to the beach? Details, please!

b-b 4 now

Mwa!

Shawn

$\mathcal{A}$fter lunch, Amanda changed her clothes and headed to the supermarket.

She hadn't felt like walking to Peichi's to get money from the treasury for supplies, so she borrowed cash from herself and Molly, and made a note that the treasury owed them money.

My third errand of the day, Amanda thought as she walked into Choice Foods. She pulled the shopping list out of her pocket and grabbed a red hand basket.

Gee! she thought. *I wish I'd been grounded. Molly's lounging in the garden, Peichi's swimming in her movie-star pool or listening to CDs in her brand-new room. Shawn's probably relaxing right now at the beach. I didn't even WANT to get into this business, and now I'm doing it all by myself. Some summer vacation this is. I wish I could take it easy today, but N-O-O! I can't! I'm too busy saving the day! Mmm...M&M's. Well, I'm just gonna buy these for myself as my little reward...and I could really use some more gum...a KitKat wouldn't hurt, either.*

As Amanda lugged the bags home, she pictured Justin

at her door. Wait—what would she wear? *Better figure that out as soon as I get home,* she told herself. Maybe she should wear her new yellow capris and peasant top...no, too dressy. She didn't want to look as if she was trying too hard...

She'd open the door and say, "Oh, hi, Justin!" as if she'd practically forgotten that he was coming over. Then she'd let him in. But what would she say then?

"Hi," said Molly, greeting her at the door. She took some of the bags from Amanda, and the girls brought everything down to the basement.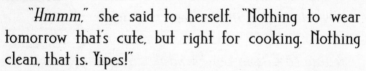

After they unloaded the groceries, Amanda ran upstairs to check out her outfit situation.

"*Hmmm,*" she said to herself. "Nothing to wear tomorrow that's cute, but right for cooking. Nothing clean, that is. Yipes!"

She picked up some dirty clothes and ran downstairs to the laundry room.

"Now what are you doing?" asked Molly, wrinkling her nose.

"Laundry, what else?" retorted Amanda. "Otherwise known as Chore Number Four."

"You don't know how to do laundry."

Molly was right. An hour later, Amanda wailed, "Oh,

no! My butterfly top! I shrank it!" She held it up to herself.

"It'll fit your teddy bear now," said Molly.

"*Aaargh!*" cried Amanda, throwing her top on the bed. "Mom's not gonna be happy about this, either."

The next morning, the doorbell rang when the girls were still up in their room.

"*Aah!*" Amanda shrieked. "It's Justin! And he's early! *Ohmigosh!*" Suddenly it didn't matter what she should wear. She threw on the first pair of shorts and top she could find and ran downstairs.

Amanda opened the door. "Hi," she said. She could barely talk, because she had to catch her breath. She smiled.

"Hi, Amanda," said Justin. He grinned. "You *are* Amanda, right?"

"Uh-huh!" said Amanda.

She led him into the kitchen. Neither of them said anything.

"Wow! This is nice!" said Justin, looking around.

"Oh, thanks."

Just then, Molly walked into the kitchen. She and Justin said hello.

"Do you want something to drink?" asked Molly. "Orange juice?"

Why didn't I think of that? wondered Amanda.

"Sure, thanks," said Justin. "So, what are we gonna make today?"

The twins told Justin the menus for Mrs. Jamison and Ms. Barlow. "We have all the recipes right here," added Amanda.

"Wow, this is a lot of food!" Justin said. "How long have you guys been doing this cooking business thing?"

He sounds impressed! Amanda thought. But before she could answer Justin, Molly started talking.

"Well, we started cooking at the beginning of the summer, but we've only done the business part for a couple of weeks," Molly said. "And it's been really crazy! We haven't advertised or anything, and new people just keep calling. I guess lots of people are too busy to cook."

"Yeah, that happens a lot at my house," Justin said. "But my brother and I usually just get a pizza!" He picked up one of the recipes. "Cupcakes? Awesome!"

"What would you like to work on?" Amanda asked him.

"Whatever you want me to," said Justin with a grin. "You're the boss!"

Just then, the doorbell rang again. It was Natasha.

"Hi," said Natasha nervously to Molly and Justin when Amanda brought her into the kitchen.

"Hi, Natasha, how are you? This is Justin," said Molly.

"Hi, Natasha," said Justin.

"Hi." Natasha smiled a shy smile and looked down at the floor.

"Have you ever cooked with these guys before?" Justin asked her.

"Yes, and we're all pretty good," Natasha replied. "Are you, um, going to Windsor Middle School in the fall?"

"Yeah! It's gonna be great."

"Okay! Let's get started," Amanda broke in. She felt weird, like she was the boss, and she didn't like it. "Who wants to make the cupcakes?"

"I will," said Natasha. She loved to bake.

"What are you gonna do with all this chicken?" Justin asked the twins.

Molly and Amanda looked at each other. "Let's make the kind we made the other day for the Falvos," suggested Amanda, and Molly nodded.

Amanda turned to Justin. "We made the most awesome chicken. And it was really easy. We just cut it up, and put it in some olive oil, teriyaki sauce, and balsamic vinegar, and threw some fresh herbs on it. Then we baked it. I think we're gonna do that. *Er*, do you know how to cut up a chicken?"

The twins smiled secretly at each other. Washing and cutting up chicken was *not* their favorite job!

Justin shrugged. "I've seen my parents do it a million times. I'll try it."

"Here's a little drawing of how to do it, just in case you need it," Amanda said, handing him a sheet of paper. "It's something we got in our cooking class." She took a deep breath. *What if Justin makes a mess of it?* she worried. *Maybe Molly and I should do it...oh, why didn't I just buy a chicken that was already cut up?*

Molly turned on the radio and began to chop the fresh herbs for the chicken.

"I'll start the plum cobbler," said Amanda.

 As Amanda washed and cut up the plums, she kept her eyes on Justin and his knife. So far, so good—he was following the instructions.

No one was saying anything.

"Justin, where do your parents work?" asked Amanda.

"My dad's an investigator—like a detective," said Justin. "We moved here from Chicago because he got a really good job here. And my mom is a designer. She designs ladies' clothes for some famous company. I can't remember which one."

"Wow! Your dad is a detective!" exclaimed Amanda. "That's cool." She giggled. "Does he wear a trench coat and carry around a magnifying glass?"

"No," said Justin, rolling his eyes. He'd heard that joke before. "You're pretty quiet, Natasha," he said.

Surprised, Natasha looked up from the cookbook and smiled.

"Were you at the beach? You look really tan," added Justin with a grin.

"I just got back from Cape Cod. I love it. We go there every summer," replied Natasha.

"Hey, I've been there lots of times! My aunt has a house there," said Justin.

As Natasha and Justin talked about their favorite places on Cape Cod, Amanda cut up her plums and wondered why Mom and Dad had never taken *her* to Cape Cod, and tried not to care that Justin wasn't trying to chat *her* up.

Molly quietly measured her ingredients and tried not to care that Justin, a boy, was in their kitchen. She really hoped that this would be the first and last time Justin would be cooking with them. Adding a boy to Dish just wouldn't be right!

"Okay, we've got the olive oil in the dish," Amanda

said to Justin. "Now coat the chicken with it, turn it over, and coat the other side...right...now, shake some of that stuff, that bottle that says 'balsamic vinegar,' on the chicken. And then the teriyaki sauce."

"How am I doing?" asked Justin, carefully shaking the liquids onto the chicken.

"Good!" replied Amanda. "I'll get the white pepper for you..." She turned away for a moment, and when she turned back, Justin was practically dumping salt on top of the chicken!

"Whoa!" she cried. "Stop!" She wanted to scream, *You're ruining it!*

Everyone looked over, surprised. Justin was turning red. Even on his neck!

Amanda forced a laugh, and said gently, "You don't need that much salt, because the teriyaki will add a salty taste."

"Whoops," said Justin. "Sorry."

"That's okay!" said Amanda, even though inside she was thinking, *Now what do I do?*

"Maybe we should wash it off and start over," she suggested. She flashed Justin a big smile so that he wouldn't feel bad. "You know, just to be on the safe side."

"Sure," said Justin. "No big." He turned on the faucet and began to wash the salt off each piece of chicken.

Just then, the phone rang. Amanda grabbed the cordless, glad for a distraction. "Hello?"

"Hi."

"Peichi?"

"Yeah, hi." There was a pause. Peichi wasn't being her chatty self.

"What's up, Peichi? We're cooking here, and kind of busy—"

"What's going on? What are you doing? I'm grounded, and I'm bored," whined Peichi. "My parents are mad at me."

It's your own fault! Amanda wanted to say. "Well, at least you're being grounded in a country club," she said. "How can you be bored there with your pool and your new room?"

"What do you mean?" asked Peichi, hurt.

Amanda took the phone up the stairs to her room. "Peichi, I really don't have time to talk right now. You and Molly didn't do Dish any favors. I had to get Justin and Natasha to help us."

"Justin! Natasha!" cried Peichi. "Wow! How'd you do that?"

"I can't *talk* now, Peichi," Amanda practically shouted. "This day is going really fast and we still have a lot to do."

"Fine," said Peichi. "Bye."

83

"Bye." Amanda heard the click of Peichi hanging up. She was still holding the phone in her hand when Molly appeared. "What are you doing?" she said. "We're really too busy for you to be talking on the phone right now."

"I know that, Molly!" Amanda replied. *Everyone* was trying to drive her nuts! "I was just telling Peichi—oh, never mind...you shouldn't be up here, Justin and Natasha will think we're ignoring them!"

Molly turned and stomped downstairs. Amanda took a deep breath and had just put down the phone when it rang under her hand.

"Hello?"

"Hi, Amanda, it's Peichi. I'm sorry! Do you want me to make a salad? I can't bring it over, but you could pick it up before you deliver all the food."

"Okay," said Amanda. "That'll help. Thanks. We'll see you later. Bye!" She hurried back downstairs.

"Peichi is making a salad," Amanda told Molly in her nicest voice. Then she walked closer to her and whispered, "Sorry!"

"Okay," Molly whispered back. Good. She and Amanda were fine.

"We just have to pick up the salad at her house,"

Amanda went on. "Hey! How are we going to deliver all this food? Mom and Dad are going to Matthew's soccer game. Well, I guess the three of us can walk it—"

Justin spoke up. "My brother Ian can drive us," he said. "He just got his driver's license." He chuckled. "It's great for me! He's so excited to drive that he'll take me anywhere I want to go—when he's allowed to use the car, that is. Can I use your phone? I'll call him."

"Sure, here's the phone," said Molly, handing Justin the cordless.

"My brother's going out with his friends," Justin told the girls after his phone call, "but my dad volunteered to drive."

"Great!" said Amanda.

"I told him I'd give him a call right before we're ready to leave," Justin said. "What do you think? Another couple of hours?"

Amanda looked at her watch. "Something like that," she said.

The girls and Justin worked hard. There was lots of cooking to do, but they finally got it all done.

When Justin's dad pulled up in front of the house, they all helped load the food into the car. Then they all piled in—all except Molly.

"So, how'd it go today?" Mr. McElroy asked as he started the car. "How'd Justin do, girls? Did he burn anything?" His brown eyes were friendly. *Justin looks a lot like him,* thought Amanda.

"So, where are we going?" asked Mr. McElroy.

"First, the Cheng's, at eighty-nine Windsor Avenue," replied Amanda from the back seat. "We have to pick up the salad there, and then we have to go to seven sixty-two Berkley Avenue, and then 5 Whitehall Place."

Peichi was waiting at the door when Mr. McElroy drove up. She walked quickly to the car, and Amanda rolled down her window.

"Hi, everybody! Hi, Justin! Hi, Mr. McElroy! Here's the salad!" called Peichi. "It's good—my mom helped me make it."

"I'll hold it on my lap," offered Amanda. "Wow! What a necklace. I've never seen you wear it before."

"It looks old," said Natasha, craning her neck to see Peichi. "Where did you get that?"

Even Mr. McElroy looked closely at the necklace. Very closely.

"That's quite a necklace, Peichi," he said. "Does it belong in your family?"

"Oh, not really," said Peichi. She'd put it on right before she'd gone out to the car to show it to her friends, but suddenly her stomach felt funny. Why was everyone so curious about where she'd gotten it? Why couldn't they just say how pretty it was?

"Well, see you later!" Peichi said abruptly, and hurried into the house.

Peichi ran upstairs to her room. She stood in front of the mirror and stared at her reflection. The pendant hung from her neck. It felt too heavy.

Because it didn't belong to her.

"*H*elloooo!" cried Ms. Brenda Barlow as she greeted the kids at the door. She was very pale, very slim, and very glamorous. She wore a sleek black cocktail dress and deep red lipstick. Her shiny chestnut hair was piled high on her head. Her long red nails matched her lipstick exactly.

"Hi, I'm Amanda—"

"Hello, Amanda! Oh, we even have a boy chef! Isn't that *cute!* Well, they say that all the best chefs are men!"

Justin smiled politely, but his face was turning beet red.

"Um, this is Justin and Natasha," continued Amanda.

"Do come in!" said Ms. Barlow, propping the door open. She led them down the hall to the kitchen, her high heels clicking and clacking on the marble floor. There stood a little girl about four years old, wearing a rhinestone crown, a frilly pink party dress, and patent-leather Mary Janes. Her hair was curled and styled exactly like her mother's. She looked surprised to see them, and a little bit afraid.

"This is *Morgan*, my little *precious*!" announced Ms. Barlow, straightening Morgan's dress. "Say hello, Morgan, like a little lady!"

Morgan gave a cute little wave.

"Hi, Morgan," said all the kids. They were still holding all the boxes.

"Oh!" said Ms. Barlow. "Just set everything right here on the counter."

This was the fun part. "Well, here's everything," said Amanda. "Cupcakes with chocolate icing and sprinkles—"

"Look, Morgan, they're for you, my precious! Don't they look *yummy*?"

Morgan didn't say anything. She just stared at the friends with her round dark eyes.

"And here's the chicken with fresh herbs," Amanda went on. "Just bake it at three hundred seventy-five degrees for about forty-five minutes. Here's the salad... plum cobbler...and roasted potatoes. Just reheat the potatoes a little bit. Okay?"

"Wonderful!" said Ms. Barlow, peeking into all the containers. "It all looks *delicious!* Thank you *very* much!" She gave them a big smile.

Aren't you going to pay us? thought Amanda.

"We need to get going," she hinted. "We have another job to deliver." *Get it, lady? J-O-B?*

"Oh, yes!" said Ms. Barlow, going to her purse. "Let me just check my pocketbook...Oh, *dear*. I *currently* have *no* cash!"

Amanda, Justin, and Natasha stared at her. Then they smiled weakly.

"Why don't you come back tomorrow, Amanda, I'll pay you then," said Ms. Barlow. "Thanks *so* much. I'll show you out. Thanks *again*. Bye-bye!"

The kids walked back to the car.

"I can't believe she didn't pay us!" exclaimed Natasha.

"'Come back tomorrow, Amanda,'" said Amanda, imitating Ms. Barlow's high-pitched voice. "Why should I go back to *her*? Why can't she come to *me*?"

"'Cause you're a kid, that's why," said Justin, opening the car door. "It's not fair, but that's always the way it is."

"What's the matter?" asked Mr. McElroy, noticing their upset expressions.

"She didn't pay us!" said Justin.

"I'm really sorry, Justin," said Amanda. "I'm so embarrassed. I'll pay you so you don't have to wait. You, too, Natasha."

"No big," said Justin as Mr. McElroy headed toward the Jamisons' house. "I snarfed down two of those cupcakes earlier. Consider me paid!"

What! thought Amanda. *Oh, no! I hope there's enough. What if Ms. Barlow notices?*

"Right," added Natasha. "It's not a big deal."

"I'm sure she'll have the money tomorrow," Mr. McElroy assured Amanda. "Maybe she got too busy to go to the bank machine. It's probably an honest mistake."

"Yeah, she was too busy—getting her nails painted!" snickered Justin. That made everyone laugh, but it didn't really make Amanda feel better. She just felt like a dumb, ripped-off kid.

"Well, at least Mrs. Jamison paid us," said Amanda a little later. "*And* tipped us." Amanda was counting the money as she, Justin, and Natasha walked back to the car. "Here you go, Natasha, and here you go, Justin."

"Hey, this is too much," said Natasha. "This doesn't leave you with anything. Here, take some money back. You can give us the rest after Brenda Barlow pays you. Really, Amanda—it's okay."

"Yeah, we'll wait for Ms. Brenda *Tightwad* to pay you," said Justin with a laugh, handing her back some money.

"Okay," said Amanda, grateful that both Justin and Natasha were trying to make her feel better.

Mr. McElroy dropped off Natasha, then drove towards Amanda's house.

Justin didn't say much after that, though he'd been pretty chatty while Natasha had been in the car.

Amanda had run out of things to say.

Mr. McElroy cleared his throat a few times.

Amanda was never so glad to see her house.

"Thanks a lot, Mr. McElroy," she said as he pulled up in front of the Moore's house.

"You're welcome, Amanda. Glad I could help."

"Well, thanks, Justin," said Amanda. "I hope you had fun, anyway."

"I did! I'll see ya later," said Justin.

Amanda gave a little wave and shut the car door.

As she walked up the steps, she saw Molly waiting for her at the front door.

"Hi," said Amanda.

"Look at this e-mail from Shawn!" exclaimed Molly, thrusting a printout at Amanda.

"You're not grounded from the computer anymore?"

"I guess not. I helped Mom weed the garden after you left, and she said I could check our e-mail."

Amanda took the paper from Molly and read:

To: mooretimes2
From: Ruth Jordan
Date: 7/23, 4:58 PM
Re:

_____

    I guess it's out of sight, out of

mind. I can't believe you guys haven't written. I sent you THREE e-mails and you never even bothered to write back.

You know where to find me if you decide you ever want to get in touch with me.

Shawn

"That's just great," said Amanda, looking up at Molly. "Shawn's mad at us."

"I can't blame her," said Molly with a sigh. "We have to write her back fast!"

Amanda sighed.

"So, how did it go, anyway?" said Molly.

"Ms. Brenda *Broke* didn't pay us."

"What!"

"Yeah, she's broke! She didn't have any cash! 'Why don't you come back tomorrow, Amanda?'" said Amanda, imitating Ms. Barlow again. She and Molly walked down the hallway and through the kitchen, out to the garden.

"Hi, honey!" called Mr. and Mrs. Moore as Amanda came out to join them and Matthew. They were relaxing before dinner.

"Hi."

"How are you, sweetie?" asked Mr. Moore. He was lying on the chaise lounge.

Matthew barely looked up. He was too busy making Kitty wear Mom's big sunglasses. As usual, Kitty was putting up with it.

"You look tired, punkin," said Mrs. Moore soothingly. She smiled her understanding "Mom" smile.

That's what did it.

"Punkin."

And the sound of Mom's gentle voice.

Mom and Dad and Matthew looked so relaxed and happy, and Amanda suddenly felt so tired and hungry and mad, that she began to sniffle, then really cry. Standing up, in front of everyone.

Amanda glanced at Molly, who was looking at her pityingly. That made Amanda cry harder.

"Amanda, honey, did you have lunch?" asked Mom, suddenly worried. She quickly handed Amanda a cracker with some cheese on it.

"No. And I've been running around and finding people to help us and m-making sure everything's o-k-kay for Dish and Justin and Natasha got along better than Justin and I did and we had to do so much today and Shawn is, like, so *mad* at us now and—and—*Brenda Barlow* didn't even *pay* us!" She began to cry again, in between gobbling down the cracker.

"Didn't pay you!" thundered Dad.

"What!" cried Mom.

"She told Amanda to come back tomorrow," Molly explained.

"She should have paid you upon delivery of all the food!" exclaimed Mom.

Well, duh, thought Molly. *Everybody knows that. Even Brenda Barlow.*

"Ms. Brenda Butthead is more like it," Matthew giggled.

"Save it, Matthew," said Mom. She patted her chair. "Sit down, sweetie," she told Amanda. "We're going to make dinner right now. Have another cracker." She hurried into the kitchen.

Amanda felt a little better after she'd had about twelve crackers with cheese.

She sat at the big picnic table in the backyard with Matthew and watched Mom, Dad, and Molly bring out dinner.

Dad's blue eyes twinkled as he set down a platter of tuna, fresh off the grill.

"You've finally reached the boiling point!" he told Amanda. "Get it? Boiling point? You're cooks—?"

The twins rolled their eyes and giggled.

"Yeah, I get it, Dad," said Amanda. She smiled at him. Dad could be so corny sometimes, but she knew he was just trying to make her feel better.

"It's not easy being a working girl, is it?" he asked Amanda.

"No, I guess it isn't." She was still sniffling a little.

"You're not just a working girl; you're a business owner," stated Mom as she set down a plate of corn on the cob. "Even adults find it difficult to run their own businesses."

Dad poured iced tea into tall glasses for Mom and himself. "You've done so well today, sweetie," he said.

"You sure have!" exclaimed Mom. "Think about it— you took the calls and accepted the jobs. You dealt with a demanding and difficult customer who changed the dates on you. You worked out a strategy for cooking food for two jobs. You hired two cooks, bought the supplies, and then had to handle this lady who didn't pay you."

Plus, I had to handle Justin, thought Amanda, *and Molly didn't even want him here. And I had to handle Peichi.*

"Wow! I rock!" she said in a perky voice, which made Mom and Dad chuckle.

Molly squirmed. All of Amanda's wonderfulness was making her look bad. She felt as if the word SLACKER were stamped on her forehead.

She cleared her throat. "I cooked, too," she said. "And I did all the cleanup after everybody left."

"And she broke something," Matthew blurted out. He grinned wickedly. "There was glass all over the floor!"

"What did you break?" asked Mom, looking alarmed.

Molly's cheeks burned.

"A measuring cup," she said, glaring at Matthew. "Nothing valuable. Sorry."

She felt the word SLACKER change to LOSER. She pretended to scratch her forehead, to make sure it wasn't really there. Molly sighed. *Why did I go to Chinatown with Peichi?* she wondered for the hundredth time.

As the twins brought the dishes into the kitchen after dinner, Amanda told Molly, "I want to go to bed. Right now. And I want to stay there all day tomorrow."

"We really need to write Shawn," Molly reminded her.

Amanda sighed dramatically. "Oh, yeah. Okay."

The twins headed into the den, turned on the computer, and began to type.

To: Ruth Jordan
From: mooretimes2
Date: 7/23, 8:34 PM
Re: sorry!!!!!!! (For Shawn!)

Hi, Shawn, remember us?

Sorry. Things have been really crazy here! Don't be mad at us, pleeeeeeze!

This is Molly. Peichi and I went to Chinatown by ourselves, and we got TOTALLY busted B/C we ran into MR. CHENG on the subway on our way home! So I've been grounded, even from the computer.

Now this is Amanda! I was grounded from the computer, 2! I had to handle 2 cooking jobs! Peichi couldn't cook cuz she was grounded 2! You weren't here! At least Molly could cook but I had to get Justin and Natasha to help us, BELIEVE IT OR NOT! And 1 customer didn't pay us!

G2G, ok? E-ya later with more deets!

b-b! BBFL

MWA!

Molly and Amanda

11

The next morning, Molly and Amanda were awakened by the squeaking, scraping sounds of Matthew practicing his violin.

"*Ugh,*" moaned Molly. She put her pillow over her head, but it was no use. "Why is he practicing so early?" she complained. "Do you think he'll ever be any good at it?"

"Are you still grounded?" asked Amanda.

"Nope."

"Good. You can go with me to Ms. Tightwad's house right after breakfast."

An hour later, Molly led the way up the steps of Brenda Barlow's brick row house and rang the bell. The twins listened for the sound of footsteps.

No one came to the door.

But Molly put her ear closer to the door and looked at Amanda with big eyes.

Amanda moved her ear closer, too.

"Sounds like footsteps," whispered Molly.

Annoyed, Molly rang the bell again.

No one answered.

"I guess she's not home," said Amanda. The twins turned and walked down the steps. As they walked away, Molly turned back and looked up.

Was someone moving the drapes upstairs?

Molly stopped walking. "I think she's upstairs!" she whispered.

"What's *with* this lady?" said Amanda. "That's it. I'm ringing the bell one more time!"

But still no one came to the door.

"What should we do?" the twins asked their parents that night.

"*Hmmm,*" said Mom. "I'm not sure. I think you should give her a few more days—"

"But do we have to keep going over there?" asked Amanda.

"Give her a call tomorrow," suggested Dad. "Ask Ms. Barlow what time you should drop by for the money."

Both Molly and Amanda wrinkled their noses.

"Oh, I hate to call grown-ups," whined Molly.

"Me, too," said Amanda. "Can't you call, Dad? Or you, Mom?"

"I think you should do it. It's good experience!" said Mom in her "peppy" voice.

The twins groaned.

"And you shouldn't feel weird about calling her," added Dad. "She owes you money!"

The twins sighed.

"I'll tell you what," said Dad. "If you don't have any luck on the phone with this Ms. What's-Her-Name, then Mom and I will help you talk to her. Okay?"

The twins nodded.

"Okay," they said.

Later that night, the twins checked their e-mail. They were surprised that Shawn hadn't written them back.

"Wow, she must be really mad at us," said Amanda.

"I know," said Molly.

"Should we write her again?" asked Amanda.

Molly shook her head. "What else can we say? We already said we're sorry. Anyway, Shawn never stays mad at us for long. She'll probably write us tomorrow."

"Hey, I know! I'm gonna send Justin an e-mail. Should I?" said Amanda.

"Why?"

"Oh, just because. I guess I want him to know that we're trying to get the money out of Brenda Barlow."

Molly shrugged. "I really don't think he cares about the money, Amanda. Besides, how do you know his e-mail address?"

"We were all talking about our e-mail addresses in the car."

"Go ahead," said Molly with a sigh. She watched over Amanda's shoulder as Amanda began to type.

To: JustMac
From: mooretimes2
Date: 7/24, 9:12 PM
Re: money

Hi, Justin, well, we went to Ms.
Brenda Cheapskate's house today and
rang the bell. She didn't answer. But
we think she was there anyway! So I'm
sory I still can't give u the $$$$.
    L8R
    Amanda

"There," said Amanda. "Do you think it's okay?"

Molly chuckled. "You misspelled 'sorry.'"

"Do you think he'll write back?" asked Amanda, typing in the other 'r' in "sorry."

"How should I know? Enough already. Just send it!"

Amanda sent it.

"Hey, here's an e-mail from Shawn! It just got here," said Amanda. She clicked on it.

To: mooretimes2
From: Ruth Jordan
Date: 7/24, 9:15 PM
Re: trouble

So, I leave town for a few days and you all turn into criminals? LOL!!! That explains why I haven't heard from Peichi, either! How did u even get Justin to cook for Dish??!! And what's up with Natasha now? Is she back in Dish or what?

My dad sent me this big package from Australia. I got a T-shirt with the Australian flag on it and a koala key chain. He even sent something for Dish—potholders with kangaroos all over them! They are so funny. My dad loves all that tourist stuff. I'm just glad he didn't send me a boomerang!

Gotta go—Grandma Ruthie needs the computer. I'll write more tomorrow.

L8R! Thanx for writing!
Mwa! <3 <3 <3
Shawn

Molly and Amanda look at each other and laughed.

"Kangaroo *potholders?*" Amanda said.

"Whatever, I'm just glad Shawn's not mad at us anymore. What a relief!" Molly said.

"I know. At least *one* thing is going right for us!" Amanda said, still laughing.

"I can't wait for Shawn to get home!" exclaimed Molly. "And for Peichi to not be grounded anymore. Things need to pick up again."

"Are you kidding?" asked Amanda. "I still need a break." She logged off the computer, and the twins went upstairs.

Early Sunday morning, Peichi called.

The Moores were in the kitchen, which was full of good smells: brewing coffee, sizzling turkey bacon, and blueberry pancakes cooking on the griddle.

"Hello?" said Amanda, answering the phone.

"Hi!" Peichi practically shouted. "I'm not grounded anymore! And we're having a big cookout today! It's for our family but my mom said I could invite you and Molly. Do you wanna come over at two o'clock?"

"Okay," said Amanda. "We're ready to have some *fun.*"

After breakfast, Molly and Amanda practiced the piano and cleaned their room.

"What are you gonna wear?" Amanda asked Molly.

"Oh, I don't know, maybe my new white shorts," replied Molly, who was stretched out on her bed.

"With what else?" asked Amanda. She frowned as she looked into the closet.

"Um, my new 'Brooklyn' T-shirt." Molly smiled. She knew Amanda didn't like that shirt.

Amanda groaned.

"Then tell me what to wear," said Molly.

"You're so lazy," Amanda giggled.

Of course Amanda tried on three different outfits before she was happy. By the time the girls got to Peichi's, it was two-thirty.

"I thought you guys were never gonna get here!" cried Peichi when she opened the door. "There aren't any kids here, and I'm so bored! Come on outside."

Peichi led the girls out to the pool area where Mr. Cheng was grilling lots of food, and Mrs. Cheng was offering cold drinks.

Molly blushed when she saw Mr. Cheng. She still felt guilty about sneaking off to Chinatown with Peichi.

"Hello, Molly," Mr. Cheng said in a friendly voice.

"Hi, Mr. Cheng," she said, looking down at the ground.

Mr. Cheng chuckled. "Have you taken any subway rides lately?"

"No," said Molly with a little laugh. "No, I've, uh, been home a lot lately."

"So has Peichi," said Mr. Cheng. His eyes were twinkling.

"Oh, Dad!" cried Peichi. "Quit teasing us!"

Peichi introduced the twins to her Aunt Doreen and Uncle Hillman, and her grandparents.

"Ah-yeh and Ah-mah, you remember Molly. Well, this is her twin sister, Amanda!" said Peichi.

Mr. and Mrs. Cheng smiled and nodded.

"Hello," said the twins. Just then, the doorbell rang.

"I'll get it!" cried Peichi. "Come on, you guys." All three girls hurried inside.

Peichi opened the door. "Hello-o-o!" she cried before the door was completely open.

It was Mr. McElroy.

"Oh, hi, Mr. McElroy!" said Peichi. She didn't know what to say. "I thought you were going to be my cousin!"

"Is your family having a party?" said Mr. McElroy. "I'm sorry, I'll come back on Monday."

Just then, Mr. Cheng came to the door. "Hello, Scott," he said. "Come on in. How can I help you? Would you care for a grilled vegetable wrap?"

"No, thanks," said Mr. McElroy. "Forgive me for interrupting your party. But I will need to speak with you very soon. Why don't you give me a call at the office on Monday?"

"Is everything all right?" asked Mr. Cheng, looking concerned.

"Well, it's—" began Mr. McElroy. He looked around.

"Please come in," said Mr. Cheng. "We can go in my study."

The two men walked down the hallway, and the girls went back outside.

"I wonder why Mr. McElroy's here?" asked Peichi. "Especially since the McElroys have already moved out of the apartment we rented to them, and back into their own house. They've been settled for a few weeks already!"

"I don't know," Molly said with a shrug. "It sounds kind of serious. Maybe Amanda can send Justin another e-mail and ask him!"

"Oh wow! You sent Justin an e-mail? What did you say? Did he write back? I can't believe you sent him an e-mail!" Peichi cried. Molly and Peichi began to giggle. Amanda blushed.

"It was no big deal," Amanda said. "I just wanted him to know I was still trying to get the money from Ms. Brenda Barlow. There wasn't any reason for him to write back or anything."

"That's too bad he didn't e-mail you back!" excalimed Peichi. "Come on, let's go put on our suits. I want to go swimming!"

Fifteen minutes later, the girls were playing "Marco Polo" in the pool when Mr. Cheng came to get Peichi.

"Peichi, come into the house, please," he said. His eyes weren't twinkling anymore. "Molly, would you please come in also?"

"O-kay," said Molly, confused.

Peichi, for once, didn't say a word.

Peichi and Molly got out of the water, wrapped towels around themselves, and followed Mr. Cheng into the house. For some reason, Ah-mah had gone inside, too.

What's going on? wondered Amanda. *Why wasn't I asked to go in?* She felt a little funny being in the pool by herself. She looked around. All the adults were speaking in lower tones and had serious expressions.

Mrs. Cheng, standing near the grill, gave everyone a big smile. "Come on over, everybody. There's lots of food here!" she called in a cheerful voice.

Amanda wasn't hungry, but she got out and went over to Mrs. Cheng, who gave her a grateful smile. But her smile didn't hide how worried she looked.

"Hello, girls," said Mr. McElroy when Peichi and Molly went into the study. Peichi's grandmother was already seated.

"Peichi, is there something you haven't told us about? Something you may have found?" Mr. Cheng asked.

Peichi suddenly went pale.

This must be about the necklace! thought Molly. *What else could it be about?*

Peichi nodded slowly. "Uh-huh. I found something."

"What was it, sweetheart?" asked Mr. Cheng.

"Um, a pendant. It looks like jade, but I don't know if it's real."

"And were did you find it, Peichi?" asked Mr. McElroy in a kind voice.

"On the floor, in Ah-yeh's and Ah-mah's store. I was going to show it to everyone, today at the party. I really was! I didn't mean to keep it a secret!" Tears slipped down her cheeks.

"It's all right, Peichi," said Mr. McElroy. "We believe you." He turned to Molly. "And Molly, were you there when Peichi found the pendant?" he asked.

Molly nodded. "Yes, sir." Molly never said "sir" but she felt that she should say it now.

"Please get the necklace, Peichi," said Mr. Cheng.

"Okay. Can Molly come with me?"

"Of course."

Peichi and Molly padded down the thickly carpeted hallway to Peichi's room.

"Am I in trouble? Am I in really big trouble?" asked Peichi as she opened her jewelry box.

"I don't know if you're in trouble," said Molly slowly. "I guess you should have shown the pendant to your grandma when you found it."

Peichi's eyes filled up with tears again.

"Don't cry now, Peichi!" said Molly in a low voice. "Let's just go back and see what's up, okay? Maybe it's not that bad!"

Peichi nodded. "You go first," she said.

She was shivering.

"Wait," said Molly. "Are you scared, or just cold?"

Peichi laughed nervously. "I don't know!" she said.

"Well, I'm cold," said Molly. "Let's ditch these wet towels. Can I borrow some sweatpants?"

The girls dressed quickly, which made them feel a little better, and Molly led the way back to the study.

"Here it is," said Peichi, handing the pendant to Mr. Cheng. Suddenly, she felt so relieved.

Ah-mah's eyes grew wide when she saw it.

"This looks quite old!" exclaimed Mr. Cheng, as he handed it to Mr. McElroy.

Mr. McElroy looked very serious as he studied the necklace. The room was so quiet that Molly could practically hear her heart thumping.

Finally Mr. McElroy spoke. "I'm almost certain that this piece is very, very old, probably dating back to the early Ching Dynasty. If I am correct, it's one of a kind—worth thousands of dollars. And it was stolen from a museum in China."

Everyone gasped.

"I've been working on this case for a while now," Mr. McElroy continued. "They moved me here to New York because I specialize in cases like this. I've been researching Chinese antiquities for months. And when I saw Peichi with the pendant, I couldn't believe my eyes! So, I did some more research and, sure enough, this pendant was reported stolen."

He turned to Ah-mah.

"I believe that smugglers are using your store to stash stolen items," he told her. "Have you seen anyone suspicious in there lately?"

Mrs. Cheng turned to her son for help, and he quickly translated what Mr. McElroy had said into Chinese.

Ah-mah looked thoughtful. She spoke in Chinese to her son.

"She says that the store is always very crowded, so it would be difficult to notice such people," Mr. Cheng told Mr. McElroy. "Luckily, there are hidden cameras throughout the store. You can look at the recent footage."

Mr. McElroy cleared his throat.

"I'll need to bring you and your husband in for questioning right away," he told Ah-mah. "This is strictly routine, you understand. And I apologize for breaking up the party."

Mr. Cheng quickly translated again, and his mother nodded her head. She spoke to her son.

"She says that she is very concerned, and that of course they will come. They will do what they can to help you," Mr. Cheng told Mr. McElroy.

"Thank you very much," Mr. McElroy said to Ah-mah. "Please take your time. We will leave when you and your husband are ready."

Mr. Cheng translated one more time, and his mother nodded.

Mr. McElroy turned to Peichi. "Thank you, Peichi," he said. "You were a big help today."

Ah-mah and Mr. Cheng smiled at Peichi, and then everyone went back downstairs.

Suddenly, Peichi turned around and ran upstairs. Molly wasn't sure what to do, so she followed her.

"Peichi, are you all right?"

"My grandparents are going to jail, and it's all my fault!" cried Peichi. She threw herself on her bed and hid her face.

Molly sat on the edge of the bed. "They aren't going

to jail, Peichi. Mr. McElroy just needs to ask them some more questions. Everything's going to be okay."

Amanda appeared at the door. "Mr. Cheng told me to come up," she said. "What's going on?"

"I got my grandparents in lots of trouble, that's what's going on!" cried Peichi. "I found a pendant in the store and it was stolen and it's a zillion years old."

"What!" said Amanda.

That's when Mrs. Cheng appeared at the door, looking very concerned.

"Hi, Mrs. Cheng," said the twins softly. Molly got up from the edge of the bed so that Mrs. Cheng could sit there.

"Don't worry, Peichi, your grandparents have nothing to hide," Mrs. Cheng said soothingly, stroking Peichi's hair. "They're not smuggling anything, and they aren't going to jail. Okay?"

Peichi was silent. Finally, she asked, "Then why did they have to go away with Mr. McElroy?"

Suddenly the twins felt that they should leave Peichi and Mrs. Cheng to themselves.

"Well, we should probably get going," said Molly.

"All right," said Mrs. Cheng. She smiled. "Peichi will call you girls later, okay?"

"Okay. Bye. Bye, Peichi."

"Bye," said Peichi without looking up.

Molly and Amanda walked down the stairs. The party was over.

"I can't believe you were with Peichi when she found that pendant," Amanda said to Molly. "Didn't you think it was real? Why didn't you tell anyone about it?"

Molly stopped walking and faced her sister. "Give it a rest, will you Amanda? Can't you see I'm upset enough over this? Why do you have to make everything worse?"

She took off down the street.

Amanda was speechless.

chapter 13

"**H**ey, Molls! Wait up," Amanda called after a minute.

Molly didn't stop walking, but she did slow down.

Amanda caught up to her. "Sorry," she said. "I know you, and especially Peichi, are really freaked out over what happened. I wasn't trying to make you feel bad. It's just that *everything's* such a mess!"

"What else is wrong?" Molly asked.

"Well, things have just been weird since Shawn left. It seemed like she didn't even care that she was leaving for a month. And then she got really mad at us for not e-mailing her. I kinda feel like everything we do is wrong," Amanda said.

Molly thought for a minute. "I know what you mean, Manda. But I don't think it's such a huge deal. Remember when Shawn went to South Carolina before? We sort of felt the same way back then, but everything was normal as soon as she came home. I think it's all gonna be fine."

"Yeah, I guess. But our business hasn't been so great, either. I mean, how can we even *have* a business when we don't get paid?"

"It was just *one* person," Molly said. "Everyone else has been paying us. And tipping us, too!"

"True," said Amanda. "But Dish has been a major stress for me lately. First Natasha bails on us, then Shawn moves away for a month, and then Peichi gets grounded and can't even help. I don't know how the two of us can do it all! I know I can't do it by myself."

Molly sighed. "I know it's been rough, Manda. But it's not going to be like this all the time. This was just a bunch of weird things happening at once, you know? Shawn will be back soon, and I know one thing: Peichi and I won't be getting grounded again anytime soon!"

Amanda giggled. "Well, I *hope* not! Because Dish totally needs you guys. Anyway, we still have to get that money out of Ms. Brenda Bubblebrain. I think we should call her as soon as we get home. And guess who's going to call?"

"Who?"

"You!"

"Me! Why me?"

Amanda giggled. "I talked to her on the phone enough when she booked us! It's your turn. Think of it as the end of your punishment."

"I've been punished enough!" Molly said. "Plus, you got something out of it all. You got Justin to help us."

Amanda looked serious. "Um, Molls? Can I ask you

something? I've been thinking about what Peichi said, about Justin not writing back...do you think that's a big deal? Like, maybe he didn't want me to e-mail him?"

"Amanda, don't *worry* so much about Justin," Molly told her. "The e-mail you sent was *fine*. Like you said, there was no reason for him to write back. It's not a big deal. Besides, we have much more important things to think about, like what's going on with Peichi's family, and getting paid!"

"Thanks, Molls. You're right." Amanda smiled sweetly at her sister. "But you're still gonna call Ms. Barlow!"

"Oh, all right," said Molly with a sigh. She knew when she'd been beaten by Amanda.

"Hey, look! There's Natasha," said Amanda, pointing to a tall figure down the street. "She's heading to our house."

"Hi, Natasha!" called the twins.

Natasha waved and waited for them to come down the hill.

"Hi, guys. What's going on?"

Amanda shook her head. "Too much!"

"Really?" Natasha asked. "What do you mean?"

Molly and Amanda looked at each other. The girls weren't sure they wanted to tell Natasha everything that was going on with Peichi's family.

"Oh it's nothing," Molly said casually. "Peichi and I aren't really out of trouble yet for going to Chinatown!"

Natasha made a little face. "That's no fun," she said. "Are you guys still grounded?"

"Um, not exactly," Molly said. "Anyway, everything will be fine." Natasha looked at the ground.

"We'll tell you all about it later," Amanda promised. "So what's up with you? Do you want to come inside?"

"Sure! Has Brenda Barlow paid us yet?" Natasha asked.

"Nope."

"Well, guess what!" said Natasha, waving some paper at them. "My dad—you know he's a lawyer—wrote a letter to Ms. Barlow for us. It's so great! You've got to read it."

"Really?" asked Amanda. "You mean, he asked for the money? Come on in!"

"I'll grab some lemonade," said Molly as Amanda and Natasha headed out to the garden.

When Molly came outside, Amanda and Natasha were already studying the letter.

"Hey! Wait for me!" said Molly, setting down the drinks.

"Look, Molls," said Amanda, pointing to the top of the letter. "Mr. Ross used his real lawyer stationery with his name printed on it!"

"It looks like he means business," added Molly. "This paper is thick. You can tell it's not just regular old paper for the printer...'David Ross, Esquire.' What does that mean?"

"I don't remember," said Natasha. "Anyway, read it!" The letter said:

T. David Ross, Esquire
Attorney at Law

July 25, 2002

Ms. Brenda Barlow
124 Carroll Place
Brooklyn, NY 11201

Re: Payment for services rendered

Dear Ms. Barlow:

My clients, the party of young cooks who own the business known as "Dish" (hereafter to be known as "Party of the First Part") have asked me to respectfully call to your attention that you (hereafter to be known as "Party of the Second Part") owe them a sum of money (hereafter to be known as "consideration"), mutually agreed upon, for cooking services rendered on or about July 23. Payment of this sum to Party of the First Part has now been in delinquency for six days. Unless payment is made within the next 30 days, a suit will be filed against Party of the Second Part by Party of the First Part in County Court on August 25 for the aforesaid consideration, plus interest.

I remain:

T. David Ross

T. David Ross, Esquire
Attorney at Law

The girls roared.

"This is great!" cried the twins at the same time.

"Though I really don't understand much of it," admitted Amanda.

"Me, either," said Molly. "But Brenda Barlow will!"

Natasha patted the envelope she had with her. "Her copy's in here," she explained. "See? Dad typed her name on the envelope. He said an envelope looks better than just sliding a plain piece of paper under her door."

"Great idea!" said Amanda. "I love this letter!"

"*Oooh*, she's gonna be so scared!" added Molly. "Thanks, Natasha. Cool idea!"

"Whose idea was it, anyway?" asked Amanda. "Yours, or you dad's?"

"Mine," replied Natasha, whose face was still red from laughing.

"What made you think of it?" asked Molly. "I never would have thought of something like this!"

"We all worked so hard that day," Natasha explained. "Plus, I think I want to be a lawyer when I grow up. I wanted to see how a lawyer would help when someone doesn't get paid."

"Let's go slide the letter under her door right now!"

"Oh, there's just one thing," said Natasha. "My dad made me promise that before we dropped off the letter, we'd give her a call. He wants us to give her another chance to pay."

"Okay," said Amanda. "But it's so awful to have to ask a grown-up for money that *we earned!*"

"I guess that's why some people hire lawyers to help them," said Natasha. "The lawyers can do the talking." She giggled. "Luckily, my dad is helping us for free!"

"I hope Brenda Barlow's not home, so she has to read the scary letter!" said Molly, cracking up again.

"Molly, you have to talk to her," ordered Amanda. "You said you would, remember? I'll get the phone book."

Molly sighed. "Oh, all right," she said.

Molly's heart pounded as Brenda Barlow's phone began to ring.

One ring. Two rings. Three rings.

Molly began to breathe a little easier.

Four rings.

"Hello!" said Ms. Barlow's voice.

Molly's heart jumped. She couldn't get any words out. But then she heard, "This is Brenda Barlow! I'm not home right now, so please leave a message—"

"Cool!" said Molly, turning off the phone. "She's not there. Let's go!"

What Natasha didn't tell Molly and Amanda was that the letter in the envelope was different from the letter she had shown them. Her father had added a little something more at the end of Ms. Barlow's letter:

Now Ms. Barlow, you and I know that these kids—including my daughter, Natasha—are not really going to sue you for what is a small sum to you and me.

My daughter came to me for help because she seems to be interested in law, but mostly because she felt that it would be awkward for her and her friends to confront you themselves. They mean no disrespect.

Would you please give this matter your earnest consideration, pay the sum requested, and get both of us off the hook? This is a great group of kids who just want to have fun and make a little money this summer. Thank you.

But Natasha really didn't want to show Molly and Amanda this part. The other part looked so official—as if they really meant business.

Natasha crossed her fingers, and hoped it would work.

123

On the way over to Ms. Barlow's house, the twins told Natasha about Peichi and the jade pendant.

"I can't believe Mr. McElroy is the detective that came over to her house!" said Natasha. "Does Justin know what happened?"

Amanda practically stopped in her tracks. With all the excitement, she'd barely wondered that herself. Why was Natasha so interested in what Justin knew?

Brenda Barlow's red brick house suddenly came into view.

"Here we are," said Amanda. "So, who wants to be the one to slip the letter under the door?"

"Not me!" said Natasha.

"Not me," echoed Amanda, giving Molly a mischievous look.

"*Aw*, why do I have to do everything?" whined Molly. "I had to call her. Why do I have to go up to the door? What if she doesn't come to the door, but she knows we're there anyway, and we slip the letter under the door, and then she opens the door really fast, and catches us?"

No one said anything for a moment.

"But then again," Molly went on, "who cares if she catches us? We have a right to ask for our money."

Amanda and Natasha nodded.

"Way to go, Molls!" exclaimed Amanda, giving Molly a high-five.

So Molly turned and went up the stairs. She walked very quietly to listen for any footsteps inside. As she stopped to listen more closely, she suddenly thought, *Oh, what the heck, I'm just gonna ring the doorbell.* She was suddenly feeling like a meanie for putting the letter under Ms. Barlow's door. What if Ms. Barlow really did mean to pay them, but just hadn't gotten to it yet? She didn't seem like a *mean* person...perhaps she was busy because she was a single mom, and here she'd planned this nice party for her little girl, and maybe she was on her way right now to the twins' house to drop off the money...how horrible it would be if she came home to this letter...or perhaps she really didn't have any extra money...maybe she'd lost her job...

"*Molly,*" called Amanda from the street. "*Hurry up!*"

Molly was shaken out of her thoughts. Suddenly, she just didn't know *what* to do. "*Ohhh,*" she moaned, quickly slipping the letter under the door. She turned and rushed down the steps.

"Let's go," she told the girls. "Now I feel bad about this."

"What?" asked Natasha and Amanda.

"Maybe the letter was—too much."

Natasha looked hurt. "But my dad wrote it," she said. "To help us."

"I know, and that's, like, so great," Molly assured her. "But maybe we should have given her more time, that's all."

Amanda's toes curled inside her sneakers. She hated awkward moments like this. But maybe Molly was right. "Do you want to come back over to our house now?" she asked Natasha.

"No, I—I can't," replied Natasha. "I have to go somewhere with my mom." She made a face. Natasha and her mom didn't always get along.

"Okay," said the twins. Natasha turned to leave.

"Sorry, Natasha," said Molly. Now she was feeling bad about what she'd said about the letter. *Ugh! Why am I always saying the wrong thing? I'm such a geek*, she thought.

"It's okay," said Natasha. She didn't seem mad this time. She waved, and walked down the hill to Garden Street.

Molly and Amanda went home and hung out in the garden with Mom while Dad and Matthew were at soccer practice. They told her about the letter that Mr. Ross had written.

"*Hmmm.* It seems a little soon for a letter like that," said Mom.

"I wonder what's going on over at Peichi's," said Amanda anxiously. "Mom, do you think something terrible will happen to Peichi's grandparents? Like, do you think they'll go to jail?"

"No, sweetie," said Mom as she watered her roses. "I'm sure everything's going to work out. Don't worry too much, okay?"

The phone rang at the Moores' house a lot the rest of that day, mostly for Mom. Not one of the calls was from Brenda Barlow.

Or Peichi.

That night, when the twins were supposed to be asleep, they were still worrying about everything.

"I thought Peichi would have called us by now!" exclaimed Amanda in the dark.

"Not getting paid by Ms. Barlow really doesn't seem very important," said Molly. "Compared to what Peichi's feeling right now."

"Uh-huh," said Amanda, turning over to face Molly. "I guess money really isn't everything."

Early the next morning, Mr. Moore woke the twins.

"Look what someone slipped under our door this morning," he said, waving a pale green envelope.

Molly rubbed her eyes.

"What is it?"

Amanda sat up in bed and reached for the envelope. "Look! It says, 'Brenda Barlow' on the return address!"

Inside was all the money she owed Dish.

"There's even a little extra," said Amanda. "And here's a note... 'Dear Dish,' " read Amanda out loud, " 'thanks for cooking such a terrific meal! Our party was a huge success, thanks to you! And little Morgan loved your cupcakes. I'm sorry you had to wait for your money. All the best, Brenda Barlow.' "

"Let me see," said Molly, reaching over to Amanda's bed. The note was written on pale green paper, edged in gold. Ms. Barlow's handwriting was large and loopy. Her signature was so fancy that it was impossible to make out her name, except for the swirly 'Bs.'

"I think you should call Ms. Barlow," said Mr. Moore.

"Why, Dad?"

"Just to say you got the money, and to say thank you. You could say that you look forward to working with her again someday."

The twins began to laugh.

"Do we really need to thank her, Dad? I mean, we worked for her, and she *finally* paid us. After not answering the door when we came over!"

"You don't know for certain that she was home then," Dad reminded the girls. "It would be a nice, and professional, thing to do. You're running a business now, and it's good to be gracious with your clients. Give her a quick call after breakfast—which will be ready pretty soon." He turned and went downstairs.

"Okay," said Molly. She looked at Amanda. "Are you gonna call her? It's your turn."

"Okay," said Amanda. She knew it was only fair.

"Here goes," said Amanda later, dialing the number. Molly picked up the cordless receiver.

"Hello?" said Ms. Barlow.

"Oh, hi, Ms. Barlow. This is Amanda Moore."

"Oh, hello, Amanda!" She sounded as happy as ever. "I slipped some money under your door this morning!"

"Yes, we got it," said Amanda. "Thank you."

"Thanks for being so *patient* with me," said Ms. Barlow. "I'm *very* forgetful! *So* sorry you had to wait for your money." She really was a nice lady, if maybe a little wacky, thought the twins.

"Well, call us if you ever need someone to cook," said Amanda. "Bye."

"I *certainly* will, dear! Bye-bye!"

Amanda sighed. "That's over with," she said.

"I'm glad you called," said Molly.

"Yeah, me, too. Let's call Natasha!"

Luckily, Natasha answered the phone. Mrs. Ross usually did, and she could be a little—stiff.

"Good news!" Amanda told Natasha. "We got our money from Brenda Barlow. Come over later and we'll give you your share!"

"Great!" said Natasha. "I guess the letter worked."

The twins looked at each other.

"I had a feeling Ms. Barlow was going to pay us soon, anyway," said Amanda. "She wrote us a really nice note. We'll show it to you."

"Oh. Maybe she's just the forgetful type," said Natasha. "See you later."

After the twins hung up, Molly asked, "Should we call Peichi? Or wait for her to call us?"

The twins decided to go ahead and call, but no one answered. The twins decided not to leave a message.

"Should I call Justin and tell him we got paid?" asked Amanda.

Molly nodded. "Sure. We owe him money."

"I sorta feel weird calling him," said Amanda. "What if he thinks I like him?"

Molly chucked. "Hello! You *do* like him."

"That's why I shouldn't call him."

"Then I'll call him," said Molly. "*I* don't like him."

"No, I want to do it! Maybe later."

BRRRIIING!

"*Aaagh!*" screeched the twins.

"The ringer on this phone is just too loud," said Molly, picking up the phone. "Hello?"

"Hel-*lo*! It's Peichi! Can I come over? Right now?"

"Okay! See ya soon."

Twenty minutes later, Peichi was sitting in the garden with the twins. "So everything worked out okay," she announced. "Guess what! Mr. McElroy and some police officers searched my grandparents' store that night of our party. They found more stuff—some old Chinese coins!"

The twins gasped.

"Mr. McElroy asked my grandparents lots of questions," Peichi went on. "And showed them photos of people whom the police are looking for. Those people stole lots of valuable old stuff from museums in China. They're using my grandparents' store to hide some of the stuff so they don't have to hide it in their

131

own homes. Then they try to sell it on the black market."

"What's the black market?" asked Amanda.

"Um, it's when you sell stuff that's illegal to sell," explained Peichi. "I just learned that yesterday. Anyway, my grandparents will keep an eye out for the bad guys. And there will be undercover cops in the store, too."

"Cool!" cried the twins.

"That museum's gonna be really glad to get the pendant back," Peichi said.

"Did you get in trouble for not showing it to anyone?" asked Molly.

"Well, I didn't get in trouble, but I sure got a *lecture*," replied Peichi. "From my parents *and* my grandma. Luckily, my grandpa didn't say anything to me. By then I think he felt sorry for me! But I guess they thought I'd been punished enough when I thought my grandparents were going to jail, so I'm not gonna be grounded." She giggled. "Again."

"Peichi, you weren't going to hide the pendant forever, were you?" Molly asked anxiously.

"No, I really wasn't," replied Peichi. Her expression was serious. "I had a big idea. I really was going to show it to my whole family, once everyone had gotten to the party." She sighed. "Lately, all my big ideas have been big mistakes!"

The girls laughed.

"We have something to tell you, too," said Amanda. "Brenda Barlow finally paid us." She reached into the pocket of her orange camouflage cargo shorts. "Here's some money for you."

"Thanks!" said Peichi. "But I only made a salad."

"You have *got* to hear what Natasha did! It's so funny!" exclaimed Amanda. "Her dad's a lawyer, and he wrote this *really* scary letter to Brenda Barlow, telling her that Dish would *sue* her if she didn't pay up! And guess what? She paid us the very next morning, before we even woke up! She slipped the money right under the front door!"

Peichi cracked up. "Natasha did that for Dish? That is so great! Wow, so Dish has a lawyer now? This business is really taking off!"

"Seriously, though, that was really nice of Natasha. She really helped us out. We should think about asking her to be a permanent Chef Girl again," Molly said.

Amanda nodded. "I think you're right. But we should talk to Shawn first, when she gets back. We don't want her to feel left out of Dish just because she's away right now."

"Yeah...Shawn got pretty upset with me for not e-mailing her! I felt really bad but at least she knows now that I was grounded from the computer. I still have to e-mail her and tell her the whole story about the pendant and Mr. McElroy and everything," Peichi said.

Just then, the phone rang. As usual, Amanda was quick to answer it.

"Hello?...Oh, hi, Justin!"

"Justin!" cried Peichi and Molly. They began to giggle. Amanda waved at them as if to say, *Be quiet! He'll hear you!*

"I'm okay," said Amanda into the receiver, as her face turned bright red. "Did you get my e-mail? Good! Well, we finally got paid, so we have some money for you... *Peichi?* Yeah, she's here. How did you know? Oh, you called her house first...Uh, sure. Here she is—"

With a little pout, Amanda handed Peichi the phone. The twins stared at her as she spoke to Justin, and she made funny little faces back at the twins.

"Hel-*lo*, Justin! What's up?" said Peichi. "...Yeah, everything's okay...No, why would I be mad at you?...No, I'm not mad at your dad! He's really nice! He was really nice to my grandparents. He has such an exciting job!...Okay, we'll call you if we ever need another cook. And we'll drop off your money...Bye!" She hung up.

"What did he say?" asked Amanda.

"He was worried that I'd be mad at him because of his dad," said Peichi.

"*Aw!* That's so cute," said Molly.

"And he wants to cook with us again if we need him."

"Wow!" said Amanda.

"Oh, really," said Molly. She didn't sound too thrilled.

BRRRIIING!

Amanda snatched the phone.

"Hello?" she said, secretly hoping it would be Justin again. But it wasn't. It was a voice Amanda had never heard before. She made a face at the others that said, *Oh, no!*

"Yes, this is the number for Dish," Amanda replied. "Oh, you heard about us from Ms. Barlow?...That's nice..." Molly and Peichi began to look anxiously at each other.

"Excuse me? I have to put you on hold for a minute," said Amanda. "Okay." She covered the mouthpiece tightly with her hand. "It's another new client!" she said.

Suddenly, the three girls began to giggle. And they couldn't stop!

"We need a break!" whispered Amanda. "Right? I know I do! Please?"

"Right!" said Molly.

"It's *unanimous*!" said Peichi, and the girls started snickering again.

Amanda removed her hand from the receiver. "Hello?" she said. "I'm sorry, we're all booked up for

now!... Right. Um, thank you for calling, though!
Bye-bye."

"Whew," said Molly and Peichi.

BRRRIIING!

As Peichi and Molly watched in disbelief, Amanda
leaned back in the chaise lounge.

She slowly sipped her soda.

And let the phone ring until it stopped.

The Amazing Cookbook

By

The CHEF Girls

AMANDA!

Molly!

Peichi ☺

shawn!

cooking tips from the chef Girls!

The Chef Girls are looking out for you!
Here are some things you should
know if you want to cook.
(Remember to ask your parents
if you can use knives and the stove!)

1   Tie back long hair so that it won't
get into the food or in the way as
you work.

2   Don't wear loose-fitting clothing
that could drag in the food or
on the stove burners.

3   Never cook in bare feet or open-toed
shoes. Something sharp or hot could
drop on your feet.

4   Always wash your hands with soap
before you handle food.

5　Read through the recipe before you start. Gather your ingredients together and measure them before you begin.

6　Turn pot handles so that they won't get knocked off the stove.

7　Use wooden spoons to stir hot liquids. Metal spoons can become very hot.

8　When cutting or peeling food, cut away from your hands.

9　Cut food on a cutting board, not the countertop.

10　Hand someone a knife with the knifepoint pointing to the floor.

11　Clean up as you go. It's safer and neater.

12　Always use a dry pot holder to remove something hot from the oven. You could get burned with a wet one, since wet ones retain heat.

13　Make sure that any spills on the floor are cleaned up right away, so that you don't slip and fall.

14 Don't put knives in clean-up water. You could reach into the water and cut yourself.

15 Use a wire rack to cool hot baking dishes to avoid scorch marks on the countertop.

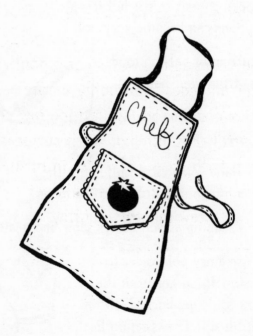

An Important Message from the Chef Girls!

Some foods can carry bacteria, such as
salmonella, that can make you sick.
To avoid salmonella, always cook poultry,
ground beef, and eggs thoroughly before eating.
Don't eat or drink foods containing raw eggs.
And wash hands, kitchen work surfaces,
and utensils with soap and water immediately
after they have been in contact
with raw meat or poultry.

WE ALL LOVE THIS, EVEN MATTHEW.
IT'S GOOD FOR YOU, AND DOESN'T
TAKE LONG TO MAKE!

—AMANDA.

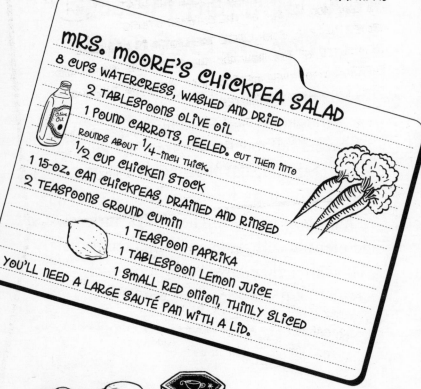

MRS. MOORE'S CHICKPEA SALAD

8 CUPS WATERCRESS, WASHED AND DRIED

2 TABLESPOONS OLIVE OIL

1 POUND CARROTS, PEELED. CUT THEM INTO ROUNDS ABOUT 1/4-INCH THICK.

1/2 CUP CHICKEN STOCK

1 15-OZ. CAN CHICKPEAS, DRAINED AND RINSED

2 TEASPOONS GROUND CUMIN

1 TEASPOON PAPRIKA

1 TABLESPOON LEMON JUICE

1 SMALL RED ONION, THINLY SLICED

YOU'LL NEED A LARGE SAUTÉ PAN WITH A LID.

HEAT 1 TABLESPOON OF THE OLIVE OIL.
ADD THE CARROTS. COOK THEM OVER MEDIUM-
HIGH HEAT FOR 5 MINUTES. REDUCE THE HEAT
TO LOW. ADD 1/4 CUP OF THE CHICKEN STOCK.
COVER THE PAN. COOK UNTIL THE LIQUID IS ABSORBED
(6 MINUTES OR SO). NOW ADD THE CHICKPEAS, CUMIN, AND
PAPRIKA. COOK OVER MEDIUM HEAT, STIRRING THE WHOLE
TIME, FOR ABOUT 2 MINUTES.

ADD THE REST OF THE CHICKEN STOCK
AND COOK, UNCOVERED, UNTIL THE LIQUID IS
ABSORBED, ABOUT 2 OR 3 MINUTES.

NOW REMOVE FROM HEAT.
ADD THE REMAINING OLIVE OIL, THE LEMON JUICE,
WATERCRESS, AND ONION, AND TOSS WELL.
YOU CAN SERVE WARM, OR AT ROOM TEMPERATURE.
OR YOU CAN MAKE IT A DAY AHEAD.
KEEP IT REFRIGERATED IF YOU DO THAT!

Mrs. Moore's
Chicken with Herbs and teriyaki
MOM JUST KIND OF MADE THIS UP! SHE'S AWESOME!

Preheat oven to 375 degrees.

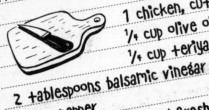

1 chicken, cut up
¼ cup olive oil
¼ cup teriyaki sauce

2 tablespoons balsamic vinegar
White pepper
¾ cup to 1 cup chopped fresh herbs
such as basil, tarragon, oregano, thyme,
or parsley. (We used a few mixed together.)
OR use 1 tablespoon dried basil and 1 tablespoon
dried tarragon if you can't get fresh herbs!

Pour the olive oil into a 9x12" glass
baking dish. Add the teriyaki sauce and
balsamic vinegar. Place the chicken pieces
in the glass dish, turning over to
coat both sides. Sprinkle a generous
amount of white pepper on both sides
of the chicken, and then the herbs on top!

Mom showed us how to put the chicken on a platter with colorful vegetables like peppers and onions. Check out mom's recipe on the next page.

—Molly

Bake it for 45 minutes. Make sure it is done. Eat it while it's warm!

You can substitute 3-4 pounds of chicken tenders or boneless chicken breasts for the whole cut-up chicken.

Sautéed Peppers and Onions

1 red pepper, 1 yellow pepper, 1 green pepper
1 whole red onion
1/4 cup olive oil
Fresh or dried Italian herbs

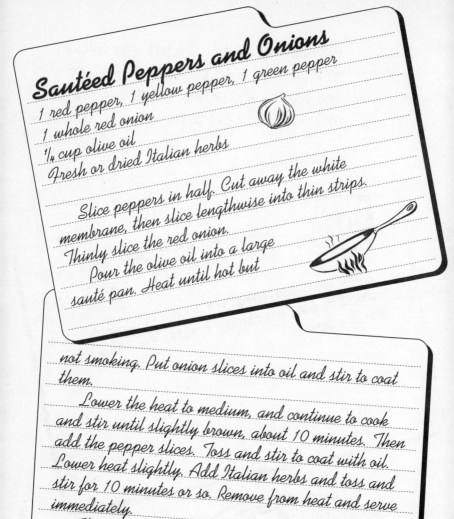

Slice peppers in half. Cut away the white membrane, then slice lengthwise into thin strips.
Thinly slice the red onion.
Pour the olive oil into a large sauté pan. Heat until hot but not smoking. Put onion slices into oil and stir to coat them.

Lower the heat to medium, and continue to cook and stir until slightly brown, about 10 minutes. Then add the pepper slices. Toss and stir to coat with oil. Lower heat slightly. Add Italian herbs and toss and stir for 10 minutes or so. Remove from heat and serve immediately.

This dish can be used to place around a platter of chicken pieces. It's simple to do, but it looks fancy!

—Mom

MR. MOORE'S
BAKED MACARONI AND CHEESE

WHEN MOM IS SICK OR OUT OF TOWN, WE ALWAYS ASK DAD TO MAKE HIS
MAC AND CHEESE! THIS IS THE WAY OUR GRANDMA TAUGHT
HIM TO MAKE IT. IT HAS TWO DIFFERENT TYPES OF CHEESE.

2 CUPS ELBOW MACARONI

1/2 CUP MARGARINE

1/4 CUP FLOUR

1/4 TEASPOON PAPRIKA

2 TEASPOONS ONION, CHOPPED FINE (THAT MEANS IN REALLY SMALL PIECES!)

1/2 TEASPOON SALT (USE PART GARLIC SALT, IF YOU HAVE IT)

1/2 TEASPOON DRY MUSTARD

1 1/2 CUPS SHREDDED CHEDDAR OR AMERICAN CHEESE

2 CUPS MILK

1/4 CUP GRATED PARMESAN CHEESE

PREHEAT THE OVEN TO 375 DEGREES.

BOIL THE MACARONI ACCORDING TO THE PACKAGE
DIRECTIONS. MAKE SURE IT DOESN'T GET TOO SOFT.
DRAIN IT AND SET IT ASIDE.

MELT THE MARGARINE IN A LARGE SAUCEPAN OVER LOW
HEAT. THEN SAUTÉ THE ONION. STIR IN THE SALT, DRY MUSTARD,
FLOUR, AND PAPRIKA. SLOWLY STIR IN THE MILK AND COOK UNTIL
IT THICKENS. ADD THE CHEESE, AND STIR UNTIL MELTED.

COMBINE THE CHEESE SAUCE AND MACARONI IN A
CASSEROLE DISH (ASK AN ADULT TO HELP YOU WITH THIS). ADD A SLICED
TOMATO (OPTIONAL), THEN SPRINKLE MORE CHEESE ON TOP IF
YOU WANT TO. BAKE IT FOR 30-35 MINUTES.

147

carmen's mom's Pie crust

this recipe is for a one-crust pie, or pastry shell.
make sure you're allowed to use the oven and stove top!

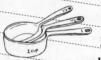

1 cup flour
½ teaspoon salt
⅓ cup plus 1 tablespoon shortening
2 tablespoons milk

You will need an 8- or 9-inch pie pan, a small knife,
a rolling pin, and if you have it, a big piece of
marble for rolling out the dough. or it can
be rolled out right on your clean countertop.

1) measure flour into mixing bowl and mix
salt through it. with a pastry cutter, cut in
shortening until mixture looks like giant peas.

2) sprinkle milk in, mixing lightly with a fork until
all the flour is moistened and sticking together.

3) gather dough together (you can use your
hands) so it cleans the bowl.

4) press firmly into a ball. wrap in waxed
paper and chill for about two hours.

5) When dough is chilled, spread on lightly floured waxed paper and pat into a round shape, by hand, then top it with another piece of waxed paper, also lightly floured. Here's a tip: take a sponge and wet your countertop under the bottom of the waxed paper so the paper doesn't slide!

6) Now, starting in the center, roll out the dough in all directions. (Don't roll too hard.) Keep turning the whole thing, and, if you need to, adjust the paper on the bottom. (You may have to lift the bottom paper and

smooth it out...if it gets too soggy, throw it out and put a new sheet on.) If you have the dough rolled out and it's sticking too much to the paper, start over with new paper and dust with flour!

7) When you have rolled the dough the size to fit the pan (it should lap over the sides of the pan), carefully remove the top paper by starting on one side, and carefully rolling it toward you.

8) Now pick up the bottom paper and carefully turn it over, to set the pastry down in the pan.

continued on p 150

149

carmen's mom's pie crust CONTINUED

Again, remove the paper by starting on one side, and carefully rolling it toward you. carefully adjust the pastry so that it's fitted at the bottom, without any tears. (But if it tears, you can patch it by pressing lightly with your fingers.)

9) Using a knife, trim the extra pastry evenly all around, leaving 1 inch to overlap. Turn under the pastry overlap

onto the top edge of the pan. crimp it with your fingers and it'll look pretty! then prick the pastry with a fork to prevent "puffing up" during baking.

10) Bake at 475 degrees for 8 minutes. If it puffs up anyway once it's in the oven, quickly (and carefully!) reach into the oven and prick it again in two places. As the pastry shell cools, make the pie filling from p 154.

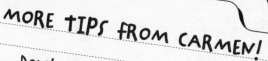

MORE TIPS FROM CARMEN!

Dough that's not chilled will be too hard to roll out. It'll stick to your work surface. But even chilled dough still sticks—and tears apart when you lift it. this is where you say, "I'M IN CONTROL HERE, NOT THE PIE DOUGH!" So don't be afraid to ball it back up. Sprinkle your hands with flour and lightly dust your work surface again with flour. (or you can even put the dough in the freezer for a few minutes!)

when starting with very cold dough, work the dough with your hands in order to make it hold together well enough to form into the round shape for rolling out. It should not be crumbly.

when you need flour, use only a dusting of flour. If you pile on the flour, the piecrust will be too tough. (A good piecrust is crumbly, not hard.)

REMEMBER: DON'T BE AFRAID OF THE DOUGH!

Chocolate Pie Filling

This recipe will be enough for a 9-inch pie.

1½ cups sugar

2½ tablespoons cornstarch   ½ teaspoon salt

3 cups milk   1 tablespoon flour

3 1-ounce squares of unsweetened chocolate, cut up

3 egg yolks, lightly beaten with fork. Have this ready in a bowl. (If you don't know how to separate eggs, have an adult help you.)

1 tablespoon butter

1½ teaspoons vanilla

Combine the sugar, salt, cornstarch and flour in a saucepan. Stir in the milk slowly and add the chocolate pieces. Cook over medium heat,

stirring all the time, until the mixture begins to bubble and thicken. Let it boil for 1 minute (keep stirring!).

Then remove the pan from the heat. Slowly pour about half the mixture into the egg yolks and beat it quickly. Then stir the warm yolk mixture back into the chocolate mixture in the saucepan. Boil for 1 more minute as you keep stirring. Remove pan from heat. Stir in the butter and vanilla.

Let the mixture cool. You can stir it a little as it cools. Then pour it into the cooled pie shell (ask an adult to help you with this if you're afraid to spill it). Chill it for 2 hours. Decorate the top with spoonfuls of whipped cream.

Everyone's gonna love this!

mooretimes2: Molly and Amanda

qtpie490: Shawn

happyface: Peichi

JustMac: Justin

Wuzzup: What's up?

Mwa smooching sound

G2G: Got To Go

deets: details

b-b: Bye-Bye

BBFL: Best Friends For Life

<3 hearts

L8R: Later, as in "See ya later!"

LOL: Laughing Out Loud

GMTA: Great Minds Think Alike

j/k: Just kidding

B/C: because

W8 4 me @: Wait for me at

thanx: thanks

BK: Big kiss

MAY: Mad about you

RUF2T?: Are you free to talk?

TTUL: Type to you later

E-ya: will e-mail you

:-@: shock

:-P: sticking out tongue

%-): confused

:-o: surprised

;-): winking or teasing

Look for these books in the Dish series!

COMING SOON...